The Big, Not-So-Small, Curvy Girls, BBW Romance, Dating Agency
Ava Catori
Copyright 2013, Ava Catori

This story is a work of fiction.

Chapter 1

"Zaftig, what is that?" Becky crinkled her nose, "It sounds like some free floating made up word."

"You could always go with chubby, chunky, or plump," Sam added.

"Just not fat, okay, because that one makes me cringe!"

"Ooh, ooh, I've got it, what about burly or the always flattering bovine!"

There was no stopping it, the dam burst as the uncontrolled laughter started. As soon as it faded, it started all over again, and through tear stained eyes, Sam shrieked, "Bovine!"

Becky gasped, "Stop, stop, my sides hurt! Can you imagine? Oh my god, oh my god, I can't breathe." Trying to catch her breath, she added, "If I go with bovine, I could use a cow for the logo. *Bovine Beauties*, it makes you want to rush right out and sign up for a date."

After the giggles died down, they tossed around more ideas. Becky was stuck on a business name. She had an idea of what she wanted, but still couldn't put her finger on the right one that would represent her dating agency.

Samantha poured herself another glass of Zinfandel. "Seriously, there's got to be something better out there. I guess the most comfortable phrase for me is plus size, but when you start to say words like large or big I panic, sucking in my gut, you know?"

Becky sighed. "Yeah, I guess *plus* isn't totally insulting. What about lush? It has a nice essence to it."

"Plus, lush, I guess one of those might work."

"Plus, plush, lush, that's it!" Becky's eyes went wide, "I think that's it, what about plush?"

Samantha ran it over her tongue, "Plush," and paused. "I kind of like it." Smiling, she held her glass up to Becky in a toast, "I think we have a winner!"

"Do you think it'll work?"

"Why not, it's got a nice ring to it. What was the other part you were thinking of again?"

"Daisies; is that too cheesy? Plush Daisies," she hesitated, waiting for her friend's judgment.

"Eh, I'm a dog groomer, what do I know? But Plush Daisies sounds kind of cute," Sam sat with the name, and then finally offered Becky a big thumb's up. "I think that might be it!"

"Oh please, you're a genius with names, Ms. Scrub-a-Dub-Doggies. Yeah, I kind of like it, Plush Daisies. It's a little different, it's cute, and combines plus and lush, it sort of has a voluptuous feel to it. I think that's it," Becky said clapping her hands. "Finally, I feel like I've been struggling with the name forever."

One bottle of wine, two satisfied women, and Becky Holgate's business plan was coming together. She knew it was a genius idea, but now she had to convince the bank. Without a loan, she'd be back to square one. Ready to get her business off the ground, this was the last piece of the puzzle. She'd finish the paperwork tomorrow, and finally apply for her business loan.

**

"What do you mean they turned you down? Holy shit, do they think fat women don't need to date? I swear that's discrimination, you should fight them," Samantha shouted into her phone, disgusted that her best friend's business was crumbling before it started.

"Screw them, it's a great idea. They just don't think I have enough background experience, and well, I guess it doesn't really matter now," she lamented.

"Becks, I think it's a great idea. You should fund it another way. Hell, I'd invest in you if I had any actual money. I'll be paying off this stupid mobile grooming van until I'm eighty."

"Thanks Sammy, but I'll figure it out. I'm not ready to give up on Plush Daisies just yet. Maybe I can take out a personal loan or something, or start it out of my house."

"That's the spirit, don't give up on it, it's genius. I've got to run; I need to fix up Franken-Fido. His owner tried to clip him herself, and let me tell you it isn't pretty."

"Right, good luck with the pup. I'll talk to you later." Hanging up the phone, Becky frowned. She thought for sure the plan would be accepted, and now she'd have to figure it out on her own. The good news was she wouldn't have a big fat loan to pay back, but the bad news was she had no idea how to pony up the cash to get started.

Heading to the freezer, Becky looked at the Double-Double-Chocolate-Trouble pint of ice cream staring her down. Determined not to go there, she turned around and grabbed her jacket. Going out would distract her, and the last thing she needed right now was calories to drown her sorrow.

She didn't mean to come home with the little ball of fur, but when the tiny orange tabby tapped the glass at the pet store, looking right at her, she was hooked. She knew it was a mistake to ask to see the kitten. Sitting with the baby cat, it mewed the sweetest baby mew she'd ever heard, and in that instant she knew the kitten was coming home with her. It just seemed like the thing to do.

"What do you think of Bella for a name, princess," she said, using a voice that instinctively went up two octaves. The soft puffball looked up at Becky, her eyes sparkling with affection and love. This was a good idea, she needed this. A sweet, innocent kitten was just what the doctor ordered. It would be nice to have a cat to bond with.

Chapter 2

"Bad kitty!" Becky scolded, as the kitten terrorized a jacket hanging on the back of a kitchen chair. Bella clung to the material with sharp, hooked nails, and only let go when she saw Becky coming. "Get off of that!"

She should have known better, that little demon of a cat ruined everything. Great, now she'd have a pull in the fabric, or precisely multiple pulls. Picking up her coat, Becky examined the damage and then put it in the closet, where it should have been in the first place.

Grabbing the phone, she muttered, "Stupid ass cat is going to ruin all my clothes," to her friend, before saying hello.

"Bella's so sweet," Sam countered.

"You mean the cat from hell? Sure, sweet if you don't count the damage she's done. It's insane, or more accurately that cat is insane. She strategically pulled all the toilet paper off the roll yesterday and then proceeded to shred it into tiny pieces all over. Do you know how long that took to clean up? There were cottony shreds everywhere. How can one little, itty, bitty kitty do so much damage?"

"Come on, she's soft and snuggly at least half of the time."

"Half, I'll give you that, but it's the other half that's driving me batty."

"She's still a baby. When all she does is curl up in a ball and sleep all day, you'll miss her fun innocence. So anyway, what are you doing tonight? I've got a bottle of wine with our names on it, and a great idea to pass your way."

"Fun innocence, yeah right, I'm aching for the days when she sleeps all day, and isn't tearing my house apart," she turned to the cat, "Yes, I'm talking about you. And yes, I'm free, what time?"

"Say seven? I've got a poodle to clip, but then I'm free."

"Sounds good, I'll see you then." Becky hung up the phone, turning just in time to catch Bella lunging from the kitchen table to the counter.

"Hey, get off of there," she said chasing her down. *Why couldn't I pick the mellow cat?*

Heading back to her desk, Becky sorted through the handful of applications she'd received. This was going to take longer than she thought. She ran an ad in the local paper asking for plus size women to fill out a form she had online. She didn't have an actual website yet, but found a free site that let her use temporary forms. After printing them out, she sat to read them. She wanted at least a pool of twenty to thirty women before she opened, but realized she might have to settle for ten. With a meager five applications, it felt fruitless. How could she offer a dating service without paying customers?

That's the part she was struggling with, how to get paying customers. She was going to offer her services free for the first three months, but if she didn't have any success pairing people up, she'd never get new people to subscribe to her service. The idea was for a plus size dating agency. If you signed up, she'd match you up with potential dates for a yearly subscription fee. Women would pay to be listed in the database, and men would sort through them and find potential dates. Of course, she'd match people together as well. The idea of a self-service website would be her goal down the line, and to build a large database. For now though, she wanted to be involved and add a personal touch.

When Samantha showed up, she came bearing gifts, wine for them and a catnip mouse for Bella. Settling on the love seat, Sam dove right in. "I sort of need a favor, Beck, but I have awesome news for you."

"Ooh, I want to hear the good news first."

"Okay, so I was doing a job today, a bath for a Jack Russell, Bean, he's adorable. Anyway, I was doing a simple bath and nail clip when I meet this guy." Sam mindlessly twirled a ringlet of hair in her finger and then let it collapse on her shoulder.

"Nice, was he cute?"

"Totally cute, but not what you're thinking. He's got a girlfriend. The thing is, I usually deal with her, but he was filling in today. Anyway, we start talking and it turns out he's a photographer on the side, sort of like a hobby he's turning into a business."

"And?"

"And, he'd said that he'd be willing to trade services. I asked him if he'd do headshots for two free grooming services."

"What do you need headshots for?" Becky reached over and picked up the wine. Corks are overrated she thought as she twisted off the cap. She got up to grab two glasses from the kitchen cabinet.

Sam's voice rose, accounting for Becky's proximity. "Not me silly, for you, so that you can look all professional when you advertise. It wouldn't cost you a dime!"

"You do that for me? What's the catch?" Coming out with the wine glasses, Becky settled back into the sofa.

"Well, remember that favor I mentioned earlier?" Her head shot to the direction of Bella, "Holy shit, look at crack kitty go," she was interrupted watching the cat tear back and forth across the room with the speed of a thoroughbred. "She loves the toy!"

"Great, now I'll have an addicted kitty and have to take her to kitty rehab. Thank your Aunt Samantha, Bella. She's the one responsible for your new drug habit." She said flatly.

"Okay, so back to the favor," Sam started. "I've got some new competition. I was in the pet store the other day picking up some supplies, and I saw this fancy circular tacked to the board. I swear they just wanted to show off their Photoshop skills," she sighed. "Anyway, I need you to go to the local stores and pull the flyers down. Just pretend like you're interested in the service, and need the paper."

"You want me to sabotage their business?"

Sam yawned, "Sabotage is such a harsh word, don't you think? I just want you to pull down a few flyers. It's for Pristine Pooches Mobile Grooming. You can do it this weekend, right?" She looked hopeful, tossing a pathetic expression Becky's way.

Becky rolled her eyes, "Fine, only because you're my best friend, but when I'm thrown in jail you'll be my first phone call, and so help me God you better show up."

"You're the absolute best. Oh, let me grab the guy's card," Samantha said. Getting up, she dug through her purse, "Here it is, Reed Amwell." Carrying the card back to Becky, she tossed it her way. "I told him your name, so he'll recognize you when you call."

"Thanks," she said, fingering the white business card. "For an artist, it's a boring card."

Chapter 3

When he answered the phone, Becky wasn't expecting the photographer to sound so sexy. She could almost feel the dampness between her legs in response to his deep voice. Holy cow, he had one of those voices that vibrated low in his chest. She almost caught herself sighing audibly. Grateful to stifle the biological response, she forced herself to speak.

"Hi, is this Reed?" She asked, reminding herself that Sam said he had a girlfriend. Not that he'd suddenly think she was the sexiest woman he's ever heard, but hey, it could happen. She pictured him with just enough razor stubble to give her goose bumps, and a wickedly handsome grin.

"Yes, and this is?"

"Oh, right, Becky Holgate. You met my friend Samantha the other day, the Scrub-A-Dub-Doggie dog groomer. She gave me your card."

"Sure, right," he said. "How can I help you out?"

Just keep talking to me. "She mentioned you could do head shots for my business."

"Of course, I remember now. What are you looking for, something candid, black and white, inside, outside," he rambled on tossing out idea after idea.

"Umm, I don't know. I never really gave it much thought. I was hoping you'd know what to do," she admitted. Why hadn't she given it more thought? Some business owner she was, not even thinking of simple little details like this.

"Sure, that's not a problem, well figure it out. Is there a better day of the week or time that works for you?"

"Evenings and weekends would work the best, but if you can only work in the afternoon, I could take a few hours off from work."

"Evenings are fine, I have a studio set up in my home. We could do it here. If you want something more natural, we could do a Saturday at the park. What type of business is it?"

Becky wasn't sure why, but her voice was small. "A dating agency," she finally said, feeling almost silly. Maybe it was that she hadn't gotten off the ground yet, or she didn't want to admit it was for curvier women, because he'd already start judging her based on her size. She hated how she always jumped there, expecting everyone to react differently to her once they learned she was bigger than what society deemed appropriate.

"Okay great, then we should be able to work in the studio. Why don't you come by one night this week, would Wednesday or Thursday work for you, say around seven?"

"Thursday should work."

After wrapping up a few details, Reed gave her directions to his home.

Hanging up her phone, Becky realized her cheeks hurt. She couldn't stop smiling. He sounded really cute, not that it mattered. She wondered if he was as handsome as she pictured.

Texting Sam, "Wow, Reed's voice! Going over Thursday for pictures, want to come?"

"Can't, have Pilates class Thursday," she wrote back. "Barely noticed his voice, will listen if I see him again."

"Hot, hot, hot," Becky reaffirmed. "Thought you were spinning or doing some kick box thing?"

"Moved on, didn't like the instructor for spinning, and felt like a failure at kickboxing."

"I need to move. I'm a slug."

"You are a slug."

"Hey!"

"A cute slug," she added to soften the blow.

"Better."

Work moved slowly that week, and Becky was convinced if she didn't get her business off the ground soon, she'd die of absolute boredom. The office she worked in was flat, bland, and beige with no sign of life, and her co-workers checked their sense of humor at the door. If it weren't for her running dialog with Sammy via text, she'd have nothing to entertain her. At least it offered a regular paycheck.

With Thursday sneaking up, Becky obsessed over what to wear for her photos. Did it really matter, they were only head shots. This was silly, it's not like it would make a difference. As long as she had her signature red lipstick on, she'd feel put together. It's like that little flash of red said she was alive, and somebody worth noticing. Not that anyone ever sat up and took notice these days.

When your curves spill over, and not in all the right places, people generally stop paying attention. She hated feeling invisible. She felt vibrant and playful inside, yet once she tipped the scale beyond cute and dainty, Becky Holgate stopped existing to plenty of men.

It's not like she even wanted a relationship anymore. She was focused on becoming a successful business woman and growing her portfolio. Financial security was her goal at this point, and she didn't need a man for that, or for anything else. *She figured if she kept telling herself the lie, she'd eventually believe it.*

It's just that all these gorgeous, vivacious, and voluptuous women were overlooked, so if she could find a way to pair them with people who would appreciate them, she'd be doing a great service. Plush Daisies was her chance to give back and create loving bonds. Okay, so maybe it would pad her income and help grow a business in the process too. Ever since she was a young girl, she pictured being her own boss. It would eventually happen, it was just going to take longer than she expected.

Following the directions Reed gave her, Becky found the place easily enough. Thankfully she wasn't too bad with directions, as long as they were clear.

She'd splurge for a GPS one of these days, but growing up locally, she knew her way around to most of the places that she frequented. That was usually enough.

Pulling her car alongside the curb, Becky turned off the ignition and slipped the key into her purse. The cute, neat rancher had manicured curb appeal. Round shrubs lined the front line of the home like squatty soldiers guarding a fort. A flower bed was just starting to bloom, and pavers created a path to the front door. Looking at the two cars in the drive, Becky wondered which was his, the sporty, red car or the four-wheel-drive. It could go either way really, a guy chasing after his ego in the sports car, or trying to feel ultra-masculine in his gritty truck. *Is it tacky to ask?* She decided to let it go, and keep her thoughts to herself.

Ringing the doorbell, she didn't expect *her* to answer. In fact, Becky had forgotten that he even had a girlfriend until the gorgeous gazelle opened the door. The woman was tall and slender, sleek, and perfectly outfitted. She easily could have stepped out of a magazine, her lips glossed, her long silky hair shining, and her clothes had the effortless look of pulled together without trying too hard.

Becky's hand went up to her chunky red necklace that she'd paired to her red lips, feeling silly. This girl was elegant and classy, and she was feeling anything but. Becky offered a tight smile. Maybe this was a mistake, head shots, what a crazy thought; she doesn't even look like a business woman.

Finally speaking after what felt like forever, "Is Reed here?"

Only she couldn't quite hear her, as her little dog was barking madly at her feet, ready to nip the hell out of her ankles if Ms.-Put-Together didn't pull him off soon. A little white and brown dog was bouncing madly in front of her, intent on letting her know he was in charge and wouldn't hesitate to act if need be.

"What?" She said, and then barked down at her dog, "Bean, stop!" The little dog pulled back long enough for her to go, "Huh?"

"Is Reed home? I'm here for pictures." *Why did she measure her own self-worth based on the people standing around her?*

"Oh, sure, right, he mentioned something about somebody stopping by."

Becky listened to her say "something about somebody"…and hated her all ready. Why? That was no reason to hate somebody. That was just stupid, but for some reason, the woman rubbed her the wrong way.

Shouting over her shoulder, "Reed, it's for you." The fashion diva didn't invite her in; she simply stood guard at the entrance with her little dog.

When he walked to the doorway, replacing the goddess, Becky had to catch her breath. She could hide the fact that her heart was racing a mile a minute, but the crimson blush that was spreading across her cheeks was visible. "Hi, I'm Becky," she said flustered, offering her hand.

"Hi Becky, it's nice to meet you. Come on inside and we'll get started." He was wearing a navy blue shirt with faded jeans, and a smile that was warm and welcoming. When she stepped in closer, she picked up a hint of Reed's cologne and quietly tried to memorize his scent. He was an exquisite package.

I'll follow you anywhere. She couldn't wipe the silly grin off her face. When he turned to look at her again, she grinned a little wider. *How embarrassing! Stop that, holy cow; you're like a schoolgirl with a crush. Keep it in check, lady.*

"We'll be working in here," he said opening the door to a back bedroom he'd turned into a small studio. "I'm still starting out, so you'll have to excuse my office."

"Oh, I know how hard it is to start a business," she lamented. "It seems like it's taking forever to get off the ground."

"It'll be worth it," he reassured. *That voice, just wow, that voice.* It was enough to leave her weak in the knees.

Reed stood six-feet tall, dreamily eight inches taller than Becky, and had the kind of shoulders a girl could lean on. She tried not to stare, but his bulging biceps peeked out from the edge of his sleeves. It's not that there were at the point of tearing his shirt, but the curved masculinity of them hinted at his strength. A firm wall of muscle seemed to be representing his chest by the way his t-shirt clung to his body. It Becky ever had a *type*, Reed Amwell was it.

See, now this is exactly what she hated. If a man was judging her based on appearance alone, she'd get angry, and here she was doing the same damn thing. How could she have one set of standards for men, and yet another for women? It wasn't fair. Slinking in, Becky realized she had double standards as the reality slapped her in the face. She was just as bad as the rest of them. She wanted to claim it was biological in her defense, but wasn't it for everybody? Well, sometimes, but maturity should get you past that!

"You can put your bag over here, and then go sit on the stool over there," he said absently pointing, while fidgeting with his camera.

Propping herself on the stool, Becky sat stiff, not sure she could put on her best face. It was hard to think of anything but the man in front of her. It was like some childish infatuation, and she was having a heck of a time snapping out of it.

"You seem a little nervous, just try to relax," he grinned. "This won't hurt a bit."

Reed adjusted the lighting and stood looking at the girl through his lens. *Something was off.* He couldn't quite place it. Her shoulders were tense, her jawline tight, and her hands were cinched together desperately on her lap. This wouldn't do, if she couldn't relax, the pictures wouldn't come out great.

Reed let his camera rest in his hands as he looked at the girl. It's like she was missing a spark. Sure she was smiling, but she seemed awkward. Trying to break the ice, Reed spoke. "Tell me about your business, you mentioned something about dating?"

How could she say it was for fat chicks? She'd be mortified; he wouldn't understand! How could he? He was an Adonis, and if she admitted it was for plus size girls like her, she'd be outing herself, and admitting out loud that she was *fat*. Who wants to do that in front of a cute guy? It's not like he couldn't see what she looked like, there was no hiding that fact, but saying it out loud felt overwhelming.

"Yep, I want to be a matchmaker," she said, her lips thin and tight, wishing she was more important. She wanted to say something impressive like that she was a doctor or lawyer, but she was simply a matchmaker, or at least trying to be one. Becky's self-judgment felt obvious.

"What got you interested in that?"

"Not getting enough dates…" she laughed, aching for a moment of clarity. She didn't mean to be so uptight sitting there, but she was stuck between nerves and the pure terror he'd realize she was fawning over him inside. "I'm kidding," *not really*, "honestly; I just like the idea of bringing two people together."

Reed smiled. She had a nice laugh; it was real, not something phony that so many women hid behind these days. It's a shame she can't relax, because when she did a moment ago her entire face lit up.

Lifting his camera, he started snapping as they talked. Looking through his lens, he noticed something – it was almost…*oh wow*. There was no tactful way to handle this.

Lowering the camera, he was about to speak when Becky jumped off the stool.

"Wow, that was fast, super, thanks so much, will you ring me when they're finished?"

"We're not finished," he said, "where are you going?"

"Oh, I just assumed," she said, "you stopped taking pictures."

Reed took a deep breath, how do you politely tell somebody there's something stuck between their teeth. "Why don't you check yourself in the mirror, and make sure everything is to your liking before I continue."

"No need, it doesn't get much better," she goaded, "besides, the sooner we finish, the sooner you can go back to your evening. I don't want to take up your time."

"Umm," he hesitated. "You may want to," he held off, and with his finger tapped on his front tooth to clue her in. He couldn't just come out and say it, could he?

"What? Not getting it, what's up?" She stared at the man as he toyed with his fingers.

Reed took a deep breath, honesty was the only way. "You've got something stuck between your teeth. I didn't notice it until I zoomed in with the camera lens. I didn't want to embarrass you."

Becky turned three shades of red, and slammed her hand up over her mouth. Not only was she sitting there talking to him, he got a close up view of food wedged between her two front teeth! She wanted to die on the spot, *die I tell you.* Becky's eyes went wide, realizing that all this time that she'd been smiling and talking, some rebel piece of food was jammed like a beaver damn in her mouth.

Talking through her hand, "Where's the bathroom?"

"Down the hall, first door on the left," he shot out behind her as she raced down the hallway.

Standing in front of the bathroom mirror, Becky stared at the offending piece of spinach. "Traitor," she ranted at the greenery sprouting in her mouth as if it had nothing better to do. How did it even end up there? It's as if the world moved in slow motion. Pinning herself to the bathroom door, she didn't want to go back.

It's just a piece of food, she groaned, it happens to everyone. Why now, why here? Taking a deep breath, she fixed herself, checked the mirror a second, third, and fourth time, and then went back down the hallway pretending like she hadn't just died a little bit inside.

"I'm sorry about that," she whispered, entering the room. She couldn't look at him. All she could picture was her stupid ass silly grin with food wedged between her teeth. Talk about making a bad first impression.

"It's not a big deal, really," he soothed. "It happens."

"Sure, to people like me," she sighed. "I'll bet nothing embarrassing like that happens to you."

"Are you kidding me?" He started laughing, "I farted on the chiropractor's table one time!"

Becky burst out laughing, "You what? Come on, now you're making stuff up to make me feel better."

"No, really, it happened. I was getting an adjustment, and there it was. It wasn't like some quiet thing you could pretend didn't happen, it was loud and obnoxious. The chiropractor tried to act like it didn't happen, she was classy like that. She was tactful and discreet, but then it lingered, you know?"

Becky's sides started to hurt, she felt the giggles rise out of her belly, up through her chest and then she was crying. Tears streaming down her cheeks, "Okay, that would more than embarrass me. I'd be mortified."

"Oh, I was horrified. We were talking golf, and there it was."

"I thought guys weren't embarrassed about that stuff," she said, grasping for air.

"Sure, with your buddies you joke about it, but it's embarrassing in front of some hot chiropractor. I mean, if I was sitting in front of the TV watching a ball game with my friends, I'd be prancing around…"

"Prancing? You don't seem like the prancing type."

Reed started laughing. "You're right, busted. I'd be fist pumping or something, prancing isn't really my style."

"Interesting choice of words," she said, looking at the man before her. He was incredibly attractive. She wished she didn't keep noticing.

"Yeah, I sort of pulled that one out of my ass unexpectedly."

"I see, so your bottom is like a carnival of excitement, all sorts of things coming out of it, fancy prance words, entertainment at the chiropractor's office," she trailed off.

Reed was grinning, this was so much better than when she first got here. She was relaxed, happy, and had a sparkle in her eye. Laughter is good for the soul.

Lifting his camera, he directed her, "Okay, tilt your chin a little to the right."

Seeing her through the lens, he noticed her softness and joy in her face. There was something special about this girl. He couldn't place it, but there was a beauty he hadn't seen when she first walked through the door. Her blonde hair framed her face perfectly, and the way her eyes danced when she laughed, it made you want to be around her without even knowing why.

Snapping the last of the pictures, he slowly lowered the lens, watching the woman before the camera. "That was great," he said, almost not wanting their time to end. What a weird feeling. It's not that he was attracted to her that way, it was just that he was enjoying their time together, and there was something else…he couldn't put his finger on it.

"Thank you so much," Becky offered. "I have no idea when my business will take off, but when it does, maybe we could work together at some point. I'd like to do professional headshots of the women I'll be working with."

"I'd like that," he said, looking at the blonde. He took note of her milky complexion and the perfect shade of red on her lips. He liked it. "I'll give you a call when the pictures are ready," he said, showing her to the door.

The little dog was back sniffing around her feet, and as she said goodbye she barely noticed the pooch. She was too busy taking in Reed's good looks to even care that the dog was about to lift his leg.

"Bean," he shouted before it could happen. Out of the corner of his eye, he caught the little dog about to mark her leg. Grateful to stop the dog before matters got worse, he said goodnight. That little dickens is always getting into trouble.

In her car, Becky exhaled deeply. "Wow." Her pulse was still racing, and she couldn't wipe the giant, goofy grin off of her face. Doing a quick check in the mirror, her teeth were still spinach free, thank goodness.

Chapter 4

"So I'm sitting there thinking he's done and I jump up. Only he's just trying to find a way to break the news to me."

"Stop, stop," she laughed. "Didn't you check before you got there?"

"Apparently not," Becky deadpanned.

"Isn't his girlfriend gorgeous?"

"Yeah, talk about feeling less than glamorous, boy I felt like a major underachiever when she opened the door."

"Yeah," Sam said, sticking her hand in the chip bag to take a fistful. "They're getting married at the end of the year."

"Married?" Becky wilted. It's not like she thought she stood a chance, and it's not like she even wanted a boyfriend, but Reed Amwell left her breathless, and the thought he'd be permanently off the market made her sad.

"Yeah, she's the one I was telling you about. She wants to do the big wedding over at Oaks." Munching on some chips, "Remember, I told you about how she was fighting with her boyfriend because he wanted something smaller, and she kept making it bigger."

"Oh! I never put two and two together." Sam gossiped with her about most of her clients. Some were friends; some were pain in the asses.

"Right, and remember I was telling you about how she said his penis was…"

Becky slammed her hands up over her ears, "Wait! Don't say it! I don't want to know." Was she afraid it would be bad news, or big news, and that just make her sadder knowing she'd never experience his…never mind.

Samantha grinned, and used her hands instead. "Big" she emphasized the length with her gestures.

"Dammit, Sam, I didn't need to know. I'm already smitten with the guy."

"Becky's got a crush," Samantha sang. "Hey, no biggie, oh wait, yes it is," she cackled.

Exhaling deeply, "Man, that guy is hot."

"You need to find some Reed types for your dating agency. Of course, you need guys who fawn over us pudgier types," she smiled. "And when you find a great one, hook me up!"

"Not as many guys are answering my ads as women are, I'm not sure where to find them."

"Maybe you should have a party, sort of a get to know what it's all about, but make it fun. You know hot strippers for the girls, poker for the guys, or at least beer. You need beer. Guys will come for free beer."

"Yes, let me just rustle up a whopping picnic du jour at the park."

"Oh, that's brilliant! Isn't there a community day or something coming up? You could set up a booth, and put out applications, sweet talk people into putting their names into a hat for a great prize. Like win a massage at the local spa, or win new tires or something for the guys."

"New tires?"

"Okay, so this isn't my strong point, but you know what I'm saying."

"Actually, it isn't such a bad idea, but I think I'll pass on the tires."

"You should call the township and get information to set up as a vendor. I'll help you. Hey, did you pull those flyers down yet?"

"A few, but I'm not sure where else to look. I snagged one at the pet store, one at the library, and one over at the market, but that's all I saw. Nice flyers."

"Hey!"

"Sorry. Crappy, crappy flyers, very unprofessional," she said apologetically.

"Right, and Pristine Pooches, please, where are we Crystal Beach? Let it go," she rolled her eyes. "The owner is probably some diva."

"Really? You see a diva washing dogs?"

"What, it could happen."

"Okay," Becky laughed, "it's just not a very glamorous job."

"Hey, it's a living."

"And a good one, but I don't see her being a diva."

"I don't know, Pristine sounds pompous if you ask me," Sam said glumly.

"So tell me what else you know about Reed, just avoid the sex stuff."

"So in other words, you want the boring details? Why do you care anyway?"

"I'm just curious."

"You do realize he's engaged to be married," she paused dramatically, "this year."

"It's not like that, I'm just curious. I might work with him when I get my business going, to do headshots."

"Sure, that's exactly what it is. Go ahead and tell yourself that."

"Shut up and pass the chips," Becky scowled. "So what, he's cute."

"Cute he is; I'll give you that."

"Besides, I don't even want a relationship. I just want to know what makes a guy like that tick. I'm trying to run a business, remember?"

"You know what makes a guy like Reed Amwell tick? A hot girlfriend," she sighed.

"Yeah," Becky joined in on the pity sigh. She wasn't the kind of girl that made him tick, and that was seriously depressing. Pushing the bag of chips away, she tossed it on the coffee table. "These are so salty, I need to stop." *Diet starts tomorrow.* But how many times had she said that? How many times had she lost a few pounds only to lose her momentum and put it all back on plus a few more? Becky's hips needed their own zip code as far as she was concerned, but starting tomorrow...okay, maybe Monday. She'd give herself the weekend to have her favorite stuff, but absolutely come Monday she was making changes.

The weekend was spent gathering details for Plush Daisies, and planning a vendor booth for community day at the park. It actually wasn't a bad idea and would get her name out there. She'd need to put together some stuff, and figure out a great giveaway to encourage people to leave their names and fill out applications. She figured if she got gift certificates for the market, and maybe one for the local spa it would be enough reason for people to leave their names and email addresses. It's not like she had a fortune to spend, but it might be just what she needed for a little more visibility.

Monday came way too soon, and life was back to its regular schedule of boring, bland, and beige. Headless co-workers lacking personality, and mundane tasks filled her time. She needed this business to work, because there was no way she could spend the rest of her existence in this "cubicle of limbo".

When she got the message that her photos were done, Becky smiled remembering the experience with Reed. What had started off as an embarrassing moment turned into laughter, and a new comfort level between them. It made the second half of the photo shoot fun. Becky crinkled her nose and giggled remembering his tale of woe to make her feel better. She'd die if she ever farted at the doctor's office. She'd have to find a new doctor, no two ways about it.

Crack kitty was sprawled across the floor, lounging with her legs wide open. She'd had a wild flinging affair with the catnip mouse, and was now worn and relaxed. Bathing herself momentarily, she collapsed back on the carpet. She swore she saw the cat humping that little catnip mouse, but let's face it at least one of them was getting some action – because Becky certainly wasn't.

Picking up her phone, she dialed Reed's number to work out a time she could pick up the pictures. She was nervous to see them, but excited to meet with him again. When he didn't answer, she stuttered trying to figure out what to say. His voice was smooth and deep on the answering machine, and as her heart sped up, she realized how silly it was. She felt like a school girl listening to his voice, and had the insane need to dial back their number a few times to keep listening. Damn caller ID, it took away all her fun. He'd know she redialed eighteen times, so she kept the thought to herself.

When he finally got back to her, he told her he could meet her the following night at the coffee shop if she was available. He kind of wanted to see her again, and didn't even know why. If she showed up to his doorstep, he'd simply hand over the photos and that would be it, and he wouldn't get to spend time with her. At least this way they could talk for a couple of minutes, maybe even think of new business ideas. There was nothing wrong with that, right?

Setting up their meeting, you couldn't really call it a date, because let's face it, he was engaged, and Becky wasn't interested, and well…it was just two people getting coffee and exchanging an envelope, right? Whatever it was, Becky was pleased that she'd get to see him one more time.

"…so you're thinking about setting up a vendor's table," Reed said, sipping his coffee. "Very clever, maybe I should do that for my photography business. I'm trying to pick up a few more clients."

"It was Sam's idea," she said, fondling her cup between her hands. "Brilliant, right? She thinks I should have a giveaway, but I'm still torn on what to give away. I have possible ideas, but I'm not sure what would draw in men. I mean, I could totally do spa for the women, but what do men want? I was thinking generic gift cards to the grocery store would be an easy option."

"Men want women," he laughed.

"Yeah, but I need them to want to date the women in my dating agency, so I can build my database."

"What guy doesn't want to meet new girls?"

"There's one tiny thing I didn't mention, and it's sort of an important part of my business."

"What?"

Becky looked down, "It's for plus sized women," she spoke softer. "And not a lot of guys want to date chubby girls."

"I see," he said. He seemed stuck. "Right, I guess some guys see that as an issue, but not every guy does." He looked at her longer than he should have.

Becky blushed, and took a sip of her coffee.

"I should be going, thanks so much for the conversation," he needed to get out of there. He was enjoying talking to this girl way more than he should be.

"The head shots are great; you're a genius with the camera. Thanks again," she said. "I'll give you a shout when I'm ready to book pictures for my girls."

"I'd like that," he said collecting his things. "It was a pleasure," he gave her a soft smile and then walked out of the little coffee shop.

Oh my gosh, he totally looked at me longer than he should have, but he totally froze up when I mentioned chubby girls. Mixed signals, she sighed. He's engaged regardless.

Chapter 5

"Look," Samantha pointed to her competition, a shiny white van sitting on the other side of the park. "Can you believe it, they signed up too." She scowled. "That's it; I'm going to have to talk to the owner. They're moving in on my territory."

"So you think dog grooming is a monopoly business?"

"Come on, be supportive."

"Sam, you can't run every dog groomer out of town."

"Fine," she sat back down, throwing her head into her hands dramatically, and pressing her elbows into the card table that Becky set up for her small vendor's area.

The booth had little interest at first, but as the day wore on, they collected a few names. Potential clients were potential clients. Each new person meant Becky and Plush Daisies had more people to work with.

A sandy-haired guy with brown eyes made his way over. "Nice giveaway," he said reading the sign. "Mind if I sign up?"

"Sure," Becky smiled, putting on her best entrepreneur face. "Have you considered joining our dating agency? I don't see a ring on your finger," she said, hoping that didn't sound too forward.

"Not married," he said filling in the details of the form, and then dropping it into the small bowl they were using to collect names.

"You should consider letting Plush Daisies set you up, we have an expanding database of women, and you might meet a great girl."

"I don't date fat chicks," he shrugged. "Sorry."

As he walked away, Becky lowered her voice, "Tear up that asshole's entry, no way is he going to win."

Samantha was looking at her.

"What?"

"Let me show you how it's done," Sam gloated, as a slender guy headed towards the table.

"Okay, Princess, more power to you."

"Hi, my name is Samantha, and you are?" She stuck her hand out, greeting the man as he made his way over.

"Brady," he said, sticking out his hand.

"You must be here to sign up for Plush Daisies, a dating agency that can help you meet a great girl, and hopefully help you find your very own happily ever after." Her voice was oozing with charm.

"Umm, actually I just wanted to drop my card off with everyone working community day. I just started a new business and I'm trying to get some exposure." As if in slow motion, he turned to point to his van, "Pristine Pooches Mobile Grooming". "I tried putting flyers up, but somebody keeps taking them down."

Samantha's mouth shut. Becky's eyes opened wide. Taking over before Sam could blow her cover, "Thanks for the card, I don't have a dog, but feel free to enter our giveaway."

"Hey, thanks. If you know somebody, maybe you could pass the card along."

"Yep, will do," Becky bit her cheek, stifling the need to burst out that she was sorry, she was guilty, but her friend Sam made her do it.

As he walked away, "So that went well," Becky said sarcastically, her voice going up.

"Damn, he's cute."

"Excuse me?"

"I wanted to not like the guy, but he's cute."

"Oh boy, here we go."

"Why do you say that?"

"Might I mention Charles, Matt, and Randy?"

"So I have a past," Sam said playfully. "All losers might I add," she groaned.

"All I'm saying is that you see a cute guy, and you jump, giving no consideration as to who he might actually be."

"You sound like my mother," Sam said, rolling her eyes. "When you were all swooning over Reed, I didn't lecture you."

"I did not swoon over Reed," Becky said, trying to change the topic. "Anyway, isn't this the business you want to take down?"

"Yeah, I guess. Ooh, sleeping with the enemy, a new tactic."

"Samantha!"

"What, he's just cute is all I'm saying. I should maybe go talk to him," she said turning away, "introduce myself, you know, in case he's new to the biz, and wants some grooming tips."

"Are you kidding me?"

She shrugged, "Cute guy takes priority," she answered, and then she was off.

Chapter 6

When Reed showed up to Becky's booth she cringed, feeling a little embarrassed. Her booth consisted of a basic card table with a homemade poster taped to it. On it there was simply a clear fish bowl with names in it for the drawing to win two gift certificates she was giving away, a clip board with a sign-up list to collect email addresses, and a few blank applications. Suddenly felt like a child doing a science experiment. The poster was childish; she should have invested more money in making the booth look more professional.

"Becky, how nice to see you here," he smiled, looking at the table. "How are things working out for you today?"

"Good," it was as if her tongue had swollen to three times its normal size, and talking took effort. It's not that she didn't want to talk to Reed; she simply got all gooey inside. "Feel free to enter the giveaway," Becky mumbled, embarrassed her community day space wasn't more impressive.

She showed up a moment behind him, "I grabbed a brochure," she walked up to his side, wrapping her arm in his, "oh, why are you stopping here?"

"This is Becky, this is the woman I was doing pictures for the other day."

"Oh, right. Hi," her enthusiasm was flat.

Becky froze, not sure what to say. It didn't help that she felt practically breathless every time she looked at the guy, but with his girlfriend standing there, she knew no matter what she said, it would fall flat.

"So what's this," she said reading the sign, and then laughing. "Plush Daisies? Is this a dating service for plus size women? Are you serious? Oh goodness, what a clever idea," she said, more poking fun than being sincere. She eyed up Becky, and felt sorry for the big girl with the small idea.

"If you know anybody who would be interested, please let them know," Becky croaked out, wishing the horrible woman would leave, but hoping Reed would stay.

"We should be moving on," Reed said, sensing Becky's discomfort. "Good luck today." He was genuine.

"Thanks," she meekly pushed out, wishing Reed's girlfriend would spontaneously combust. Okay, so maybe not something so violent, she didn't have to combust, maybe she could just melt and dissolve right into the ground, disappearing forever, she wasn't picky.

As Reed and his fiancée walked past, Becky couldn't help but stare at them. They were gorgeous together, and it was obvious what Reed saw in the girl. She was a knock-out, like seriously beautiful, the kind of woman you look at and instantly think she must model on the side. Becky felt two sizes fatter after the woman showed up. It didn't matter that she hadn't actually gotten any bigger, next to somebody like that, she immediately felt less attractive. She hated how she let those thoughts swirl in her brain, but there they were, and it's not like she could ignore them no matter how much she wanted to.

Samantha finally found her way back, "I gave him some tips, and we're going to try to work out some territory boundaries so we don't step on each other's toes too much. He's actually a pretty nice guy. He's going to work the area more west of the highway, since I have a lot of customers here in-town and to the east."

"Wow, all that from one conversation," Becky said, stunned.

"I get right to the point," she smiled.

"Do you think he'll actually do that, just stick to the west side?"

Sam shrugged, "It couldn't hurt to ask; besides we can talk about it more over dinner. We're going to grab a bite to eat and share horror stories and clients to avoid."

"Dinner? Seriously, how do you do that so fast?"

"What?" She laughed.

"It's just that you're so comfortable talking to guys. Why do you want me to set you up, you have no problem meeting people."

"I don't need you to set me up; I just want you to set aside any good potential guys for me to date first, before passing them on to other girls if I'm not interested."

"Ah, so like a priority list. You get first dibs?"

"Exactly."

Becky laughed, "You'll scare away all of my clients before I get off the ground."

"Oh nice, Becks, I'm not that bad."

"No, you're right, everybody goes zero to sixty in four seconds."

Sam grinned, "I know what you're saying, but I can slow down if I want to."

"I'd love to see you try," Becky challenged. "Hey, Reed and what's her face came by earlier."

"Oh yeah, your kissy face boyfriend. You're in love," she teased, her voice playful. "Did you gush all over him?"

"You're a child."

"That's why you love me."

Becky rolled her eyes.

"How much longer are you going to stay?" Sam settled back into the chair alongside her friend.

"I think it goes until three. I'm going to stick here until the end. I've got nothing to lose, just time. I don't think it's going very well, but at least I got a handful of names."

"You've got to start somewhere, Becks, it doesn't happen overnight."

"I know," she sighed, "but I desperately want out of my other job."

"Who can blame you? I'd rather poke myself in the eye with a fork than work a cubicle job."

"Do you think I could ever get a guy like Reed?"

"Sure, why not?"

"I don't know, I'm just not feeling very pretty right now."

"Becky, you're adorable, and there's so much more to you. You're sweet and funny, you're smart, and you have good taste in friends," she grinned. "No seriously, I hate how you think you can't get certain guys. You really limit yourself, because you have this wall around you that screams insecure sometimes."

Sucking in her cheek, Becky looked at Sam. "You think it's obvious, or is it because you know me?"

"Look at your body language, your arms are all tight to your chest, you're closed off."

Becky quickened loosened her arms, "I'm not closed off."

"You sort of are. You're afraid something good might happen."

"That's ridiculous; I want something good to happen."

"You say you do, but your actions say something else."

Becky looked at her friend, "I've been hurt, I can't help that I shut down. Jeremy used to tell me how I'd gotten fat," before she could finish, Sam cut her off.

"Jeremy was two years ago," she soothed. "It's time to let go of that pain, hon."

Becky nodded. "You're right."

"You're letting some asshole's words rot in your brain. Stop letting some guy that isn't even important in your life make you feel bad about who you are. For the record, he's a jerk. You are a viable, smart, sassy woman. Now start acting like one."

"Thanks, Sam. I needed that today."

She nodded in understanding.

When Reed came back, sans fiancée, Becky was surprised.

"Hi," she said, his smile radiating perfect teeth. It was almost as if the sun was gleaming off of them. Could the guy get any better looking? She was amazed how every single time she saw him, her heart raced and she felt breathless. She'd never been so attracted to a guy before.

"Reed!" Becky was surprised to see him returning to her booth. "Can I help you with something?"

"I was actually thinking I might be able to help you."

"How so?"

"Do you have a website for your new business yet?"

"Not quite, but I hope to put one up soon." She had no idea how to do it actually. She'd either have to pay someone, and didn't have the spare cash, or she'd have to learn to do it herself. She'd stared at tutorials, and gotten nowhere fast. Clearing her throat, trying to sound like she put more thought into it, "I didn't want to advertise it before I had enough people in my database."

"I do web design, nothing fancy mind you, but I'd be able to help you get set up if you'd like."

"Wow, that's so nice of you. I don't have much of a budget, unfortunately. I was going to maybe get one of those quickie free pages."

"Nonsense, I can help you put up a simple, professional site, and help you get started."

"You'd do that?"

"Sure, maybe you could put a link on your site to mine in return for payment. Sort of like, I use Reed Amwell for all my photography needs."

"Wow, that's genius, which would be great. I wouldn't mind at all," her words spilled out too quickly. Why it that she either spoke too fast, mumbled, or could barely get out words around this guy? Becky tried to meter out her words, so they sounded almost normal. "I'd love that, thanks so much."

"No problem. You have my card, why don't you give me a call next week and we'll set some time aside to work on the design you have in mind."

"Okay, great," she couldn't wipe the smile off her face. It was so big that her cheeks hurt.

That's when *she* came back; Miss-gorgeous-model-girlfriend walked up. "I'm ready to go," she sighed. "That chair massage at the spa booth was fabulous."

Becky knew she should have hired someone to do something like that! Trying to break the ice, "Congratulations, I heard you're getting married." She hated saying the words out loud, but she couldn't think of anything else.

"Yep," she looped her arm around Reed's. Pulling him away, "This fall, can't wait."

"Thanks again," Becky called out as they started to walk away.

"Holy shit!" Samantha's mouth hung open. "He came back, I think he likes you."

"What are you talking about? He's getting married."

"Why would he offer his services out of the blue like that?"

"Maybe he just wants to help, or to get word about his business out too. Stop jumping to conclusions, it's not like that. He was just being nice."

Sam shook her head slowly. "Becky Holgate, I think Reed is interested in you." She stared at her friend, stunned by the turn in events.

"Oh stop it," she said, blushing. "That's ridiculous." *Could he like me?*

Chapter 7

Reed wasn't sure why he went back. He convinced himself it was to network and to make a good contact. Besides, helping her get her business started seemed like a nice thing to do. It's not like it would cost him anything but time. He'd just help her set up a basic website. It was almost crucial to have a website in this day and age if you wanted to be taken seriously. Besides, he could link back to his photography site and help grow his own side business in the meantime.

He convinced himself that's all it was.

When Jessica mocked her, he felt almost defensive, not even knowing why. Was it really necessary to use that tone with the girl? She was trying to start her own business; Jessica didn't have to be so cold toward her. He thought it was a good idea. Sure it wasn't a dating agency he'd frequent, but he was sure plenty of guys would. Maybe he'd ask some of his single friends if they'd be interested in helping her get started. Scowling, he realized it probably wouldn't go over well. The first thing his buddies ask about a girl is if she's hot. His friends didn't generally go for chubby girls.

Reed suddenly felt shallow. Did he and his friends only care about looks? That was crazy; he wasn't like that was he? He wanted to believe he liked people for who they were. When he stopped to actually question himself, he saw how quickly he shut out the idea of dating somebody larger, and yet he was drawn to Becky for some reason. She was soft and sweet.

What if a friend was trying to set him up on a blind date, and he described the girl as chubby? He'd stop his buddy there and shut it down. Let's face it, his looks afforded him the cream of the crop, and he usually only settled for gorgeous women that other guys drooled over.

Reed's stomach turned at his reality. He did judge people by their appearance way too quickly, and yet he was attracted to Becky. She wasn't his type, and it's not like he wanted to go out with the girl, he just thought she was cute. She felt real. He hated seeing this side of himself. It was usually tucked away, not something he thought about, and now that it was staring him in the face he wasn't feeling very good about himself.

Shaking his head, he realized he was fighting an uphill battle. Here he was trying to convince himself he'd date fat chicks, when he knew damn well he'd never once dated a girl that was chunky – not once. So why was he drawn to this blonde cherub that smiled and made him want to be around her?

He was happily engaged, ready to be married to a gorgeous girl. Okay, so he wasn't totally thrilled about being off the market completely, and it really had been her idea. She was ready way before he was, but they'd been dating for such a long time, and it was time for him to man up and finally make the ultimate commitment. He just wished he was more excited.

She was over the moon when he asked, but something deep inside told him she might not be *the one*. He loved her, they were good together, hell, they'd been living together for the last two years, but something was missing. He couldn't put his finger on it, but he always thought he'd be certain when it came time to propose. Instead, he did it because he felt obligated. It was the next step in their relationship. First comes love, then there's marriage, and then kids…he froze at the thought. He wasn't ready for kids. He wasn't ready for this.

What he did know is that he loved Jessica. The moment he saw her, he knew he had to have her. He pursued her like every other guy on campus did, but she chose him. She used to make him weak in the knees and want nothing more than to spend every waking moment with her curled up in bed. It was such a strong biological response, he couldn't even deny it. Only after so much time together, they'd grown comfortable with "good enough", and he wondered if that's what married life would be like.

Would he never feel the spark again? She'd be his *one and only* for the rest of his life. Was that enough? Reed felt almost guilty thinking like that, but he was a man, and some days he couldn't help himself. Usually it was just a passing glance at a nice set of legs, maybe a great rack, but it was never more than a quick look. He didn't take it further, never tried to make more out of it than that. He loved Jessica, and had no urge to go elsewhere – only even with all of that, there were still the tiniest bits of doubt creeping in. Maybe it was cold feet, who knows, but he hated that it stayed with him.

His interest in Becky took him off guard. She wasn't the kind of girl he'd ever be drawn to, but for some reason, she drifted into his thoughts time to time. It's not like he wanted to throw her down and make mad passionate love to the girl, it wasn't that kind of response. It was more that he wanted to spend time with her, talking, listening to her laugh, and watching her milky complexion flush, her cheeks turning a pretty shade of pink. What was that? He barely knew the girl, barely spent time with her, but still she sat on the edge of his brain.

Whatever it was, he needed to knock it off, because it wasn't doing him any favors. Speaking of favors, he told her he'd help her with her business website. Maybe that wasn't such a good idea. If he spent more time around the girl, it would be harder to forget about her. He tried to shift his focus back to Jessica and their wedding, but the soft, curvy blonde he'd met recently was stealing more and more of his attention.

Chapter 8

"How is this even possible?" Becky stared at her inbox. She'd gotten four more applications, and counting the ones from community day, she now had close to fifteen women interested and two men. It was a start, though she'd need more guys to get things moving. At least she could try to get the two guys matched up. Scanning the applications, she groaned at the answers one guy left behind. Okay, so at least she had one decent application. She tucked the second application aside for desperate times. Even with so few applications, she wasn't that desperate yet. Some things are better left unsaid. She looked it over again and flinched. Yep, we'll just tuck this into the "better off not dating this century" file.

When the phone rang, she absentmindedly picked it up, while still scanning the applications. "Hello?"

"Hi Becky, it's Reed."

Catching her breath, she responded as calmly as possible. "Hi, how are you?" Her heart kicked into high gear.

"I'm good, thanks. I wanted to see if you had time this week to talk about a vision for your web page."

"A vision," she suddenly felt stuck. She really hadn't put as much time into it as she thought she did, because when it came down to it, she kind of didn't know.

"Yes, like what type of information you'd like available, what you want your main page to look like, if you want it to look edgy and current, comfortable and homey, or were looking for a more business feel, very upscale and clean."

"Wow, I don't really know."

"Do you have a logo, or colors you'd like to work with?"

"Umm," she froze up. What had started as an iota of an idea was fading from her brain. "Maybe I'm not ready for this yet," she said, anxiety creeping in. Was it anxiety over her business, or was it that Reed Amwell, the guy that made her feel all gooey inside was on the phone. She wanted to sound sharp and well thought out, but instead went into a panic.

Her pulse was racing, her palms were sweaty, and all Becky wanted at that moment was to get off the phone. It's not that she didn't want to talk to Reed. It's that she wanted to do more than talk to Reed, and that thought alone was rushing through her brain at full throttle. As her words choked in her throat and her mind seized, she was stuck.

Out of nowhere, Bella went tearing across the room and slammed into a vase sitting on a side table, "Bad Kitty!"

"Bad kitty?"

"I've got to go," she spurted out and hung up. "Dammit Bella," Becky said, going to clean up the mess, and in that instant realized she'd just hung up on the very guy she not only had a crush on, but was willing to help her create a website. No, no, no, she didn't mean to. Should she call him back and apologize, or has the moment passed?

She quickly checked the caller ID and redialed his number.

"Hello?" Reed answered half curious, half amused on seeing her number pop up on his phone. "Is everything okay?"

"I'm sorry," she said, rambling. "Listen, I really appreciate you wanting to help me, I just don't know where to start and it overwhelms me. You overwhelm me. I mean," she startled herself, she didn't mean to blurt that out, and then she kept going, "I'm sorry, I didn't mean that in a bad way, it's just that I seem to freeze up when you're talking to me, and I don't know what's wrong with me, and I feel like a fool, and…" her words were getting faster and faster, and soon she was tripping over them.

Reed interrupted "Breathe."

Becky took a deep breath. Exhaling, she admitted, "I want your help, I'm just not sure where to start."

"Why don't we start with a basic piece of information? You know the name of your company, but have you designed a logo yet? Will you be using a logo?"

"I had a basic idea, but I feel silly. I'm not very artsy, as you could tell from the amateur poster at my booth the other day, but I'm not really sure how to start."

"Why don't we start with your logo? I can help you. What were you thinking of?"

"I was thinking of a white daisy with the petals outlined in blue, a yellow center outlined in red, and then the words of the company maybe in the petals, in the center, or as part of the stem and leaves. I'm kind of torn on that part."

"It's a solid idea. Why don't I sketch a few ideas and you can see if you like one?"

"Why are you helping me? This is so sweet of you, but you really don't need to."

"I want to help you. You seem like a nice girl, and it's a good idea."

"Okay," she sighed. "I'd really like the help. I feel stuck."

"Why don't I meet you over at the coffee shop one night this week, and you can see if any of the designs appeals to you, and from there we'll discuss colors for your website."

Becky wasn't sure how it was possible, but once again she was on the way to the coffee shop to meet Reed, the very man that made her dizzy with excitement, made her heart race like a thoroughbred, and left her breathless with lust.

Before running out of the house, she checked the mirror one last time. Smiling, there was no sign of spinach, no sign of life, and no sign of a small beaver damn between her teeth. Feeling content with a final check, she headed out the door. It was so sweet of him to be doing this for her. She was excited to see the designs he sketched out. It was pure luck that he was so good with creative stuff, and that he was offering her to help. What are the chances?

Pulling up, she was giddy on seeing his truck. The very SUV that had been sitting in the driveway that first night she met him. She was glad he had the truck and not the sporty red car. It was an ego car, and he didn't seem like an ego person, he felt more down to earth. His girlfriend, now she seemed like the flashy type that liked eyes on her. Yep, his truck was here because he wanted to talk to her, help her, and spend time with her.

Walking in, she smoothed her skirt down in the front and scanned the room. He waved on seeing Becky. Feeling her anxiety kick in, she talked herself down. *Keep calm, act professional, don't trip, don't make a fool of yourself, and simply offer your hand as a friendly gesture.*

Reed stood to greet her, and as he spoke she smiled graciously, forcing herself not to jump his bones the second she heard his voice.

"Becky, it's great to see so much of you. I think the rest of the coffee shop is happy to see so much of you too." Lowering his voice, "Your skirt is tucked up into the back of your panties."

Dying would have been too painless. If Becky could have single handedly plucked the nails embedded in the hardwood floors, and skimmed the planks off the floor, she would have gladly crawled under a board and had Reed hammer it back into place.

Reaching down, her brain frozen in time, she felt for and then found the offending piece of material that was wedged into the backside of her panties. How had she not felt the breeze, holy cow, how many people saw, and as her fingers went to her rounded thigh, she reached up and yanked down the fabric.

She couldn't breathe, each breath felt shallower and shallower, and as her pulse quickened, her breathing went with it. Trying to gain control, she forced herself to count each breath, *no, no, you're not allowed to panic, breathe.*

"Are you okay?" She heard the voice in the distance. Before her was beautiful Reed, gorgeous, handsome, attractive Reed looking directly at her.

Shaking herself out of it, slowly regaining her composure, she stopped before going into full blown hyperventilation mode. "Yes," she said flatly, "I think I need to sit down."

"Of course," his hand was wrapped around her waist, helping her back onto one of the overstuffed chairs. His hand was touching her, holy cow, don't let go.

Blinking, she took in the scene. Reed was standing over her, and in a moment of total exhaustion, she felt it rise up from her belly. There was no stopping it, and though she felt like she might be sick from the traumatic embarrassment, a fit of nervous giggles spilled out of her like a pot of boiling water that couldn't be controlled.

Horrified, her face completely flushed with what could only be described as total humiliation, Becky Holgate laughed like there was no tomorrow. Caught up in the moment, Reed laughed with her.

When the tears started, she couldn't stop them. Not only had she made another absolutely miserable impression on the guy, she looked like she couldn't even dress herself. *Sure, why not...why the hell not?* The laughter slowed to a trickle, and then started back up again. Reed wasn't even sure what he was laughing at anymore, but her laugh was contagious, and soon he was grasping at his sides, trying to catch his own breath.

"Holy shit," she started, when a horrible goose like honk came out of her. The laughter went from normal to weird noises and then there was no noise, just air as she was gasping for breath, and before she could stop it, a goose honking sound again.

Reed bent over laughing harder on hearing the obnoxious honking. And then it happened, with all the laughing there was no control, Reed farted in front of the entire coffee shop. Becky lost control all over again, honking, wheezing, crying, and screaming with laughter. They were quite the pair.

Everyone was staring, but Becky couldn't help herself. She was in pain now, and desperately needed oxygen. Did he really just do that, oh my god, her skirt was tucked up in her underwear, what the hell? Finally, after they couldn't laugh any more, they sat side by side in two chairs and looked at one another. It started with a small giggle, but then erupted into total chaos with more tears, more honking, and more uncontrolled laughter.

Becky was the first to speak, barely able to catch her breath. "So, I can't be trusted to dress myself, and your bottom has quite a reputation for being vocal," she started. "And here I thought I looked all classy in my new skirt," she sighed.

Reed smiled. "Your skirt is great, but your laugh is amazing," he said, looking over at her, unable to look away.

Becky turned away, blushing. "Thank you."

"Can I get you a cup of coffee? I have the designs for the logo here."

"That would be great, thanks."

"I'll spread them out here, and you can look at them while I go get your drink." Reed pulled out different images he sketched out, and laid them side by side.

Becky moved to the small sofa and scanned the designs spread before her. They were incredible. He'd taken her thoughts and created visuals that got her excited. They were all fantastic. She'd have trouble deciding which she liked the best.

Returning with Becky's coffee, Reed sat beside her on the small sofa. "What do you think?" He asked, handing her the beverage.

"I love them," she turned to look at him, and as he looked up, she knew she was in trouble. Their eyes met, and sitting only inches apart, she looked at his lips.

He couldn't pull himself away. He knew he was too close, he should move, this isn't right, and yet he was stuck. This was wrong, back up fella, you're going to get in trouble, and as his eyes lowered from her gaze to her lips, her eyes following his, he leaned in closer, his lips about to brush against her own – when he finally stopped himself. Righting himself, he quickly stood, realizing how close he had just come to cheating on his fiancée, how close he'd come to kissing the girl before him, and how much he desperately wanted to kiss the girl sitting beside him.

Becky inhaled slowly, taking in the scent of Reed's cologne, the smell of gods, masculine and strong, and as he inched in closer, his lips about to touch hers, she closed her eyes. Only he didn't kiss her, instead he pulled away and jumped up – and everything inside of her collapsed. She desperately wanted him to kiss her, but knew it was wrong. He belonged to another woman.

The silence was deafening.

Becky cleared her throat, "I like this one," she said, pulling one particular sketch aside.

"Right, great," Reed felt off balance. He wanted to sit with her, run the back of his hand across her perfect milky complexion, and then let his fingers rake through her soft, blonde hair. He wanted to touch her, feel her, and pull her into an embrace. Instead, he needed to get out of here, and fast.

"You're welcome to use it," he said quickly. "I don't think I should work on this project. I'm sorry to have put you in this position."

"Please don't apologize," she started. "I shouldn't have intruded on your time. I appreciate your help, but you've done enough for me. Thank you so much," she said, standing with her coffee. "I should be the one to go."

Turning to leave, Reed spoke softly. "Please don't go yet." He knew it was wrong, but he wanted to spend more time around the girl. She made him smile inside. He was afraid if she walked out the door, he'd never see her again.

"I can't do this," she said, putting on her big girl panties. "Reed, you're amazing, but I'm feeling things I shouldn't feel. You belong to somebody else." With that, she turned and left.

Sitting in her car, she caught her breath. He almost kissed her. She would have let him, she wanted him to, and yet he wasn't even available. Not like he'd leave Ms. Gorgeous for her, but for a single second, she felt like he was attracted to her and everything inside of Becky soared – until she looked in the mirror, and understood that fat girls like her don't land guys like

Reed. It was a moment, he was caught up in the adrenaline of laughing, and it was nothing more.

The tap on the window startled her. Looking up, she saw Reed. Rolling down her window, she shyly greeted him. "Hey."

"I need to apologize. I was out of line. Anyway, I wanted to give you these sketches. Maybe you could use one of them. If you bring them to a printer or designer, they can work with them and make one into something you may want to use. You're welcome to them. Again, I'm sorry. I crossed the line," he said. "Drive safely," he added before turning to go to his truck.

Becky watched him walk to his truck and climb in. She didn't want him to leave, but what she wanted didn't matter. He was engaged to be married, and that meant he was off limits. Obviously they had a moment back there, but that's all it was, a moment.

Turning her key in the ignition, she carefully pulled out of her parking spot and headed home. What if he had kissed her? What would she have done? Would she have kissed him back, pulled away telling him it was wrong, or…she knew the answer, and pretending like she'd do anything but kiss him back was just a big, fat lie.

She wanted to taste his lips, feel his warm mouth on hers, and run her fingers through his dark hair. She wanted to touch him, press against his solid body, and melt into his arms. It wasn't even a kiss, it was a near miss, and that's all it would ever be. But just like every other encounter with Reed, he left her breathless, absolutely breathless.

It had been a long time since she'd fallen so hard. Jeremy was the last man to steal her heart, but then proceeded to stomp on it and shatter it into tiny pieces. She recognized the feelings she was having, and this was no ordinary crush. This was something more, only it didn't really matter, because Reed Amwell was off the market.

Jeremy Gramble was her college sweetheart, even though she'd initially fallen for his twin brother Josh. She'd mixed them up, and after having a crush on Josh, she accidently bumped into him, or what she thought was him, and they got to talking. When she literally tripped over his foot, and he helped her up, they immediately started a rambling, confusing conversation. Mistaken identity turned into true love, however crazy that may seem, and in a twist of fate, she found out that Jeremy was the Gramble for her, and not Josh.

But that was beside the point, Jeremy was her past, and Reed couldn't be her future, because he belonged to somebody else. What Becky needed more than anything was to focus on her business, because she didn't want a relationship, even if she did think Reed was about the most handsome man she'd ever laid eyes on. She wanted to be self-employed, be her own boss, and make other women's lives better, so for now, men and dating were off her mind, and it was all business all the time, because there's no way she was going to waste another second thinking about a man she couldn't even have.

Chapter 9

Becky couldn't call Sam fast enough. She was torn between telling her everything and telling her scraps of details. It's not that she didn't trust Sam, it's just that her best friend had a way of blurting out information at the wrong time, and Jessica and Reed were her clients.

"So, he almost kissed me," she started before Sam could say hello.

"Who almost kissed you?" Sam seemed distracted, out of breath.

"Reed!"

"Shit, really? Did you kiss him back?"

"I said almost," Becky paused. "What are you doing?"

"Who am I doing," she corrected. "Can I call you back in a few minutes?"

"Fine," she sighed. Becky was disappointed; she wanted to dissect her evening with Samantha. Figures she'd have bad timing.

The phone rang twenty minutes later. Sheepishly, "Sorry, I was busy."

"Who was it?"

"Yeah, that's not important," she said changing the topic. "Reed? Tell me all the details."

"Not much to tell. He drew some logos for me, I went to meet him, and he almost kissed me."

"Back up, it's like there's a giant gap in there somewhere."

"Fine," Becky took a deep breath. "I went to meet him, and I totally screwed up. My stupid skirt was shoved up in my panties, and…"

Sam interrupted, "What?"

"Yeah, that's not important, just one of my usual mess ups, so anyway, it's totally awkward and I start laughing. You know how I get nervous giggles; well this blew up into ugly laughing, with goose honking and tears…"

"Oh, tell me you didn't honk," she shot out. "Not the honk."

"Yes, the honk," Becky confirmed, "so anyway, I'm dying, and he starts laughing, and the next thing you know he farts," she paused to let that sink in.

"He farted? Oh, gross! Go on," she said, now hanging onto every word.

"Right, but we're laughing so hard, and he can't help it, well this sends us into fits of giggles again, and next thing you know we're sitting near each other and…"

"Did it smell?"

"Oh my gosh, really?"

"What? It's a legitimate question. Dude farts, you're standing there, you're talking about kissing, so I'm wondering are you really grossed out, like does it stink, or is it just loud, you know the kind that sound dangerous, but really doesn't do nasal damage."

"You're impossible, Sammy! Just let me tell you the story."

"Fine, go on, leave out important information. I'm just saying it won't be as complete of a story is all, if you don't fill in the details."

Becky huffed, "Fine, it didn't stink, it was just loud."

"That's embarrassing," she answered.

"Right, so anyway, we finally settle down, he goes and gets me coffee then sits down next to me, like really close. I look over and he's looking over, and he leans in. I closed my eyes, thinking he was about to kiss me, and then nothing."

"Nothing?"

"Right, he panics, jumps up, and I rush out. Anyway, he almost kissed me, I totally wanted him to, but now it's all weird and he's not going to work on my web page."

There was silence, and then a quick gasp.

"Sam, are you there?"

"Yeah," she was quiet again. "I need a moment." Sam talks to somebody in the background. "Give me just a second," she whispers.

"Becky, I absolutely want to discuss this with you, but Brady is between my legs and I can't focus. If you could just hang in there, I'll call you back, but he's getting impatient."

"Oh my gosh, are you having sex? And you called me back? I thought he left!"

"No, not sex this time. We already did that. He's giving me oral," and then she started laughing. "Yeah, okay, I'm totally busted. I need to go; I'll call you when Brady leaves. I wanted to hear about it, but it's totally not a good time."

"Brady, like the dog grooming guy?"

"Yeah, him, got to go," and with that she hung up.

Becky sat staring at her phone. *Unbelievable*.

Sinking into her sofa, Beck replayed the events of the evening through her mind. What would have happened if he didn't stop, if he followed through and kissed her, then what? Closing her eyes, she tried to imagine how his kiss would have felt, and what he tasted like. She could almost sense it, lifting her fingers to her lips, Becky sighed. She really wanted him to.

When the phone finally rang, she braced herself, "Is he still there?"

"No, I sent him home."

"So soon?"

"Eh, he's cute, but I don't want a relationship with the guy."

"So you'll sleep with him, you just won't date him? Nice standards," she mocked.

"I'm not sure if I'll sleep with him again, he's just sort of okay. I may have screwed up. I mean, he's nice and all, but he wasn't that great in bed. It wasn't bad or anything, but I didn't feel a spark."

"Are you going to see him again?"

"We'll see. I'll think about it, but I don't think he's my type. He's a little vanilla for my taste."

Becky shook her head, "Does he know you're kicking him to the curb?"

"He's not still here is he? I told him I don't do clingy, and I needed my space."

"How did he take it?"

"I think he was relieved, actually. We had fun, but we didn't really click."

"But you still slept with him?"

"What's your point?" Sam argued.

"Okay, we'll discuss your less than stellar choices later. Let's talk about Reed!"

"Yeah, that kind of surprises me. Not that he could be interested in you, but that he'd almost cheat on Jessica like that."

"What do you mean?"

"He doesn't strike me as the cheating type."

"It's not like it was planned," Becky got defensive.

"I don't mean it like that, I mean, if he's drawn to kiss you, maybe he likes you."

"You think? I'm wondering if it was just the high of the moment."

"Maybe, but he does keep coming up with reasons to see you. I think he likes you."

Becky couldn't help but smile, "Really?"

"I don't know, but what else could it be?"

"I don't know," Becky sighed, "but whatever it is, that guy floats my boat. He's so damn hot, my hair singes every time I see him."

"Just be careful, Becks, I know how you get."

"What's that supposed to mean?"

"Really?"

"Okay, fine," Becky admitted defeat. Maybe she did get a little obsessive when she liked a guy, but not in a scary way, just in the way that she talked about him non-stop, and that wore down everyone around her.

"So what are you going to do?"

"I'm not doing anything. It was one time, and now we go our separate ways. Besides, I have a business to focus on," Becky stated.

"How's that going?"

"I need a favor," she started.

"A favor?"

"Yeah," Becky paused, thinking about how to phrase the next part. "I have this guy who put an application in, but I have some concerns. I was wondering if you'd go out with him one time and give me a read on the guy. Is he date worthy, or is he creepy."

"Sure, throw me into the fire," she laughed.

"Come on, please do this for me. You're courageous," she grinned.

"You owe me," she sighed.

"Hey, I pulled Brady's flyers down, the same Brady you just slept with by the way."

"So what's wrong with the guy, the one you want me to date?"

"He's a little forward," she said, trying to buffer the blow.

"Forward?"

Becky gave in. "Okay, the part of the application that asks why you'd be interested in dating a plus sized girl, he said and I quote, *chubby girls with big asses turn me on*," she groaned. "Right on the application, he didn't pull any punches."

"Wow, cut to the chase."

"Exactly," Becky sighed. "The only thing is I don't have a lot of men to pull from, and I'm kind of desperate. So I need to know is he creepy, or is he just not tactful in how he writes things down. Like maybe he thought I wanted to know what his exact thoughts were, I don't know. I don't want to make excuses for him, but I have next to nobody to set my girls up with."

"Okay," she agreed. "I'll do it, but you still owe me."

"You're the best," Becky squealed. "His name is Jonathon. I'll tell you more next time I see you. Hey, what are you doing this weekend?"

"Obviously not Brady after assessing his oral skills, and probably not Jonathon; I vote we get a bottle of wine and a movie, and stay in."

"Sounds good, want to come over for dinner?"

"Sure, let's say five. You can fill me in on all the details, and I'll tell you about my non-date with Brady."

"Deal."

Tossing her phone on the table, Becky got up to change into something more comfortable. Pulling her hair up, she slid on her pajama pants, and went to wash her face. Seeing her reflection in the mirror, she touched her lips thinking of Reed. *He almost kissed her, almost.*

This is silly; he'd never go for a girl like me. Becky pouted noticing how round her cheeks were. Turning to see her profile, she frowned seeing her fullness. This is depressing. Walking out of the bathroom, she plopped back down onto the sofa. The clarity she had earlier was fading, and all that was left was her disgust with her shape and size. She was more than a number on some scale; she was a smart girl, ready to launch her own business, so why did she feel absolutely glum and undesirable, when just moments before she was soaring on the thought that Reed almost kissed her?

There weren't any answers that satisfied her in this current mood.

The rest of the week was uneventful and paled in comparison to her time with Reed, but with the weekend finally here, she'd get to relax and have some fun. Samantha was on her way over with a movie and a bottle of wine, and Becky had put together full of crockpot of meatballs for sandwiches later.

Stirring in the sauce, she drifted off thinking about Reed once again, and like some bad penny that followed her around, her low self-esteem followed right behind it. He doesn't date girls like you, besides he's engaged, and it's never going to happen. It was a vicious cycle of maybe he could like me, that's silly, he can date anybody he wants and he chose some model-type, not a fat, fleshy girl.

When Sam showed up, Becky was relieved. The distraction was exactly what she needed. Reed was the only thing on her mind lately, and it was getting old.

"So," she dropped onto the sofa, "tell me about this guy you want me to check out."

"His name is Jonathon. He's in his late twenties, seems like he has a solid business background, has been with the same company for a couple of years, but he's kind of rough around the edges, a little crude in his answers. I don't know, it gave me a creepy vibe, but I'm not sure if it's just that he was tacky, or if it's more than that."

"Throw me under the bus," she laughed, "sure, I'll go out with him one time. I'm like some kind of test porpoise, throw me in the water and see if I float?"

"You're so good at stuff like this."

"Stuff like what? I've never done this for you before."

"You know what I mean. You're really outgoing, and good at reading people. I'm desperate; I need more guys to sign up. I've got a nice portfolio of women, but I don't want to send them out with icky guys, you know?"

"But you'll send me out with one?"

"You talked to me while Brady was between your legs performing oral sex on you," Becky said flatly.

"Point taken, I'm flexible," she winked. "So when do you want me to do this?"

"The sooner the better," Becky smiled sweetly. "If he's a go, I'll have two guys and can start setting a couple of girls up to see if I can find a match."

Sam exhaled dramatically, "The things I do for you."

"You're the best," Becky grinned. "Here's his application," she said, shoving it across the table to her friend.

Sam scanned it over, "You owe me big."

"Yeah, he's a little rough around the edges."

"Chubby girls with big asses turn me on?"

Becky shrugged, "So he's not Prince Charming."

"He's not even the frog."

"Will you still do it?"

"Yeah sure, why not," she sighed.

"You're the best."

"I know."

Chapter 10

Samantha was smitten, "I think I'm in love."

"What?"

"Jonathon," she sighed, "he's really good in bed."

"What? You were supposed to date him, not sleep with him!"

"I know, I know, but wait until you hear about our date."

"Go on," Becky was nervous, this wasn't the plan.

"Well, he took me to this really nice restaurant down on Main. We should go there sometime; I didn't even know it was there. Anyway, we start talking, and his foot is rubbing against my leg, and a few glasses of wine later, we're full on making out at the table. We finally pay and leave, but he's got me pressed to his car, his kisses passionate and sweet, and he's nibbling on my neck. Beck, you know how that gets me going, so anyway, we finally make it into the car, and can barely leave the parking lot. His hands are hot and heavy, and I'm feeling good, I've got a nice buzz going, and then we end up back at my place. Seriously, that boy's got moves. We were naked and before I knew it, we were panting and exhausted under the covers. It was amazing, and holy shit, it was insane. He wasn't shy, he certainly didn't hold back, and wow can he use his tongue."

"Okay, too much information! Are you going to see him again?"

"Hell yes. I'm not letting this one slip away."

"Well, at least I made a match," Becky sighed, "even if I didn't mean to."

"He's actually really sweet and funny. He said he figured he might as well be honest on the application, so he didn't waste anyone's time."

"All rightly then," hmm, where would she find other guys?

"There's just one little thing," she whined.

"What? Does he live in his grandmother's basement?"

"Oh please, as if I'd go on a second date with him if that were the case, it's just that he has a weird laugh."

"A weird laugh?"

"Yeah, it's more feminine than masculine."

"What?"

"I know, I know, it's not a big deal, but I swear he sounded like a girl giggling, instead of a guy."

Becky laughed, "This is your issue?"

"It's stupid. I'll get over it, but otherwise, total package."

"Well, glad it worked out, but now I'm down another guy."

"I'll help you come up with an idea to get more guys. You still have that one guy left, right?"

"What if he hits it off with the first girl?"

"You'll have made a match!"

"But I'll have run out of guys!"

"What were you going to do, send him on a cycle, going out with each girl?"

"I don't know, but how can I be a matchmaker without more guys?"

"You need to get that website ready, that way you'll have more of a presence."

"Yeah, I guess. Reed was going to help me, but now I'm going to have to hire someone."

"Or you could learn to do it yourself."

"I'm not good with creative stuff," Becky lamented.

"Maybe you've improved, you don't know if you don't try."

"Think professional, I'll hire someone."

"I can ask around and see if anyone I know does them."

"Hey, glad it worked out for you."

"Thanks," Sam said.

Becky could almost hear her smiling.

When the text came through the following day, she wasn't expecting it. Sitting, holding her phone, she wasn't sure what to do. Should she text back?

"I've been thinking about you." It was such a small sentence, and yet the joy that shot through her on reading it was intense. Becky's breathing quickened, and her heart started to pitter patter, realizing whose name was attached to the message.

Should she respond? Is this a mistake? She sat looking at it, wondering if he was waiting for her to say something. Should she play coy, be direct, or ignore it, and pretend like she didn't see the message. Engaging in a response would mean she acknowledged the thought. Playing with responses, she finally went with a simple, "That makes me smile." *Was it too much, not enough?*

Her heart felt like it might leap out of her chest, and as she waited, watching for something else, nothing came. It felt like seconds turned into hours, and staring at her phone, she willed it to do something – anything.

Finally another message came through. "Can I see you?"

Becky's hand shot up to her mouth as she gasped. The smile that spread across her face was immense as she typed back, "Yes". *He's engaged; due to be married, this is a mistake. Holy shit, I'm a home wrecker.* Her breathing got deeper, and sitting staring at her phone, she realized she was shaking. *He wants to see me.* There was nothing more in the world that Becky Holgate wanted than to see Reed one more time.

"Coffee shop, eight tonight?"

"Okay." That's it, she's doing it. The reality was sinking in. He contacted *her*. He wanted to see *her*. This was his idea. She sat in disbelief for a few minutes and just as she was about to share the news with Sam, decided to hold off. Becky loved Sam, but she wasn't very good with secrets, and the last thing she needed was for her to mention it to Jessica if she ran into her.

Becky spent the entire day thinking about what she'd wear, and made a mental note to scan her body up and down multiple times. No beaver dam in her teeth, make sure her skirt isn't wedged in her girly bits, in fact wear slacks, and dear goodness make sure there's not one single embarrassing thing going on with her body.

Becky glared at the clock, aching for time to move faster. This was going to be the world's longest day. She must have checked the clock hundreds of times over the course of the day, and as it finally got to the point where she could leave work, she rushed back to her house to dig through her closet. She knew exactly what she was going to wear.

Gliding the red lipstick over her lips, she refreshed her make-up. Checking and double checking in the mirror, everything passed her approval. Picking up her perfume, Becky sprayed a bit of the floral scent on, before pulling her boots out of the closet. She'd chosen sexy black boots to go with gray slacks that flattered her round shape. Pulling on a silk white blouse, she grabbed a charcoal gray blazer and slipped it over her blouse. Spinning in front of the full length mirror, she made sure everything was where it should be, and then skipped out to her car.

He really wants to see me, she sighed. Me.

Pulling up to the coffee shop, Becky felt her pulse sprint at the sight of Reed's truck. He was here, inside, waiting for her. Is this a mistake? Once she goes inside and admits there's something between them, there's no way to take that back. What does it mean? He's still engaged, right? It's not like it means anything. *I'm certainly not interested in some secret affair, and it's not like he's ditching his soon to be bride for me....why I am here?*

Becky checked herself in her rearview mirror, and got out of the car. Standing in the parking lot, it took everything inside of her to get her feet moving. She was glued to the ground, afraid of seeing him again. She knew it would leave her breathless and wanting more. What was the point of tonight anyway?

Slowly, she put one foot in front of the other and found herself at the entrance. Reaching up, she pulled the door open and took one final deep breath. It's now or never.

Glancing across the room, she saw him. Her heart quickened. She swore he got better looking every time she was near him. When he looked over and recognized her, his face lit up. Smiling, he stood to walk over and greet her.

There was an awkward moment where they didn't know whether to shake hands, give a friendly hug, or just say hello. "It's nice to see you," he finally said, breaking the silence.

"And you," she said. Her cheeks hurt from smiling so big.

"Thanks for coming to see me," he started. Becky followed him to the area he'd chosen. "What can I get you?"

"A cup of tea and a croissant would be great, thanks." She sat watching him place her order. When he returned, he sat beside her nervously.

Thanking him, she exhaled and hoped he'd start the conversation. She wasn't sure what to say. She was thrilled to see him, but what's the point. When he started talking, she was relieved.

"I can't stop thinking about you," he admitted. "You're adorable, and have the best smile," he said, "and your eyes, they flicker when you're laughing, sparkling like gems. I sound goofy," he laughed quietly, "like a schoolboy with a crush."

"You're sweet," Becky said blushing. "But you're also engaged to be married," she added softly.

"I know," his voice was low. "The thing is, I'm attracted to you, and I'm not sure what to do about that."

"I wish I could help you. It's just that I don't date men who belong to other women." She hated saying those words out loud. She wanted to tell him she was all his, but knew she couldn't. If there was one thing she wanted to hold onto, it was her integrity, and Reed belonged to Jessica. He'd pledged his love to her, and asked her to be his wife.

He looked at Becky, watching her face, watching her lips, wanting to taste them, and then leaned back into the sofa. "I'm so confused."

"There's nothing to be confused about," Becky said, placing her hand on top of his. "You've got a lovely fiancée, and I'm sure she'd appreciate you respecting her." She took a deep breath, "Besides, I'm not interested in a relationship." *It was a lie, a big fat lie*. If Reed would have her, she'd be with him in an instant, but not like this. Not when he belonged to another.

"You don't feel this, what's going on between us?"

Becky caught her breath. "Reed," she couldn't get out another word. Looking at the man beside her, she had nothing else to say.

Leaning toward Becky, Reed moved in closer, space closing between them. Becky watched him, now inches away, and as he was right before her, he whispered. "I want to taste you."

Becky swallowed hard. Their lips were almost touching, barely any space between them. She wanted to remain strong, needed to turn him away, but her resistance was waning.

She could feel his hot breath, and as her breathing slowed, time stood still. Lingering in the moment, she held fast.

He whispered again, "To touch you, to taste you, to kiss you."

Becky's heart was beating faster than she could fathom, and finally whispered back, "Kiss me."

His lips brushed up against hers, barely touching, and in that moment she snapped back to reality. Pulling back, "Reed, I can't do this."

He nodded quietly. "I'm sorry; I just needed to see you. You're constantly on my mind."

"I'm flattered," she sighed, "but until you're single, I can't do this. You've got a wedding to attend."

Reed looked at Becky. He felt shame wash over him. With a simple apology, he got up and left.

Becky watched him walk away. It was heartbreaking, but there was no other way.

Chapter 11

At precisely eleven o'clock, Becky's phone buzzed. Rolling over, she picked it up hoping it was Reed saying he'd made up his mind and was choosing her.

"Jonathon's available," came across her screen.

"I thought you liked him." Becky sat up in bed and texted Samantha back.

"Can I call?"

"Yeah."

Her phone rang seconds later. "It's his laugh," Sam said.

"Seriously?"

"Yeah, I can't get past it. He laughs like a girl."

"You're impossible. You meet a guy you like, and then let go because of one tiny thing."

"If you heard him, you'd understand. He'll be good for your dating agency though, he's a good guy. Just not for me," she threw in at the last minute.

"Okay." Becky debated. Should she tell her? It could backfire, but if she didn't tell her, she might burst. "I saw Reed tonight."

"What?" Sam's voice went up. "What happened?"

"He almost kissed me again. He said he keeps thinking about me."

"Wow."

"Yeah," Becky said.

"And?"

"I told him he belonged to somebody else."

"How do you feel?"

"I'm confused. I'm really drawn to the guy. He's incredible in every way, but there's that one small detail, he's freaking engaged!"

"Oh Becks, I'm sorry honey."

"It's okay, I'll survive."

"Jonathon is available. Hot sex might make you feel better," she laughed.

"Very funny. Anyway, I need to sleep. I'll talk to you in the morning."

"Yeah, I should probably sleep at some point," she groaned.

Becky tossed and turned. She couldn't stop thinking about Reed's words, his mouth so close, and his hot breath on her. Tracing her lips slowly, her fingers followed the soft, pouty line of her lower lip.

Becky's fingers slid off her lips, traveling along her neck, and quietly crept lower. Drawing them across her chest, she cupped her breast, wishing it was Reed's hands on her. Her breathing slowed, and with lazy, calculated movements, Becky let her imagination run free. Moving her hand down to her naughty bits, she pleasured herself. With a small gasp, she drifted on the high of the orgasm she gave herself. Sleep followed soon after.

On waking, she curled into her covers, not wanting to leave the comfort of her warm bed. Work was the last thing she wanted to do today. Tossing around excuses and reasons to call out, she sighed and accepted her fate. Climbing out of bed, Becky relented and took her shower.

If only she could stop thinking about Reed. Standing in the shower, drying her hair, making breakfast, it didn't matter the activity, she still heard his words. "I want to taste you," and felt his hot breath, his lips barely inches away. Not that it mattered, he belonged to somebody else.

Reed stood under the hot water, letting the shower spray around him, drops of steam and mist filling the air. Adjusting the temperature the slightest bit, he sank into the increased heat. There was nothing Reed liked more in the morning that a hot shower. It used to be that a morning romp with Jessica was his favorite past time, but lately they'd let things slide. Mornings became a routine of coffee, newspapers, and showers – and barely talking. It's not that things weren't great, they were, but after so much time together, they'd developed patterns.

When she first moved in with him, they couldn't get enough of each other. It was like the beginning of their relationship all over again, and the sex was non-stop and hot. There were so many reasons to adore Jessica, she was a great catch, and the sex had always been amazing, but lately something felt off. They didn't make as much time for each other, and she was always fussing over wedding details.

Holy shit, did he get tired of the details. He didn't care if the napkins were chardonnay or pink or rose or whatever shade she was obsessing over. He didn't care if they had baby shrimp on their salad or water chestnuts or what type of lettuce was used. He just didn't care. When he pictured getting married, he pictured how it would feel, not what the table centerpieces would look like. Yet, that's all she seemed to care about lately, and she'd bury him with the details constantly.

Should she wear her hair up or down, and how many bridesmaids, and you should do this, and don't forget to do that. It's just not what he pictured his wedding to be. When he asked her to marry him, he thought the joy they felt would be captured on their wedding day. A few friends and family, something small, intimate, romantic, and most of all would be a celebration. This felt more like some formal affair where love was left at the door. It's not what he pictured at all. They'd already fought about the wedding more times than he could count on one hand, but it made Jessica happy being buried in those details. Sometimes he wondered if she wanted him, or simply wanted some grand wedding.

On meeting Becky, he never expected the girl to capture his interest. It was really a passing thing at first, but she kept bouncing through his mind when he least expected it. It wasn't planned, but there she was again, smiling, laughing, her bright red lips, and her bouncy blonde curls. She was real, and had this adorable awkwardness that made him smile.

Reaching down, he took his hardness in his hands. Her soft curves made him hungry for her. A quick release and he was ready to start his day.

Climbing out of the shower, Reed toweled off and went to get dressed. When Jessica smiled at him seductively and asked him if he wanted to climb back into bed, he made an excuse. He had a meeting to get to, *and that's when he knew*. This wasn't working for him anymore.

It's not that he didn't love Jessica; Jess was all that and the whipped cream too. It's just that after so many years, it felt more like the next step, rather than what he wanted in his life. When he saw forever, he wasn't sure what he saw. Some days it was Jess, other days it wasn't. There was a lot of guilt associated with that. He'd asked her to marry him, he committed, but maybe he did it for all the wrong reasons. It seemed like the thing to do, she was getting impatient, but why didn't he feel like he was certain?

Why was he suddenly attracted to a woman that wasn't even his type? Why did he feel the need to be around her? Sure, he'd been attracted to girls before, but not like this...*this was different*. This was more. He couldn't place it, but he wanted to be around her, almost like when he first met Jessica. The intense urge to spend time with her was something he couldn't let go of. The idea of ignoring Becky Holgate seemed impossible.

He wasn't done watching her smile, he wasn't done laughing with her, and he wasn't done wanting to kiss her. He wanted to run his fingers through her hair, and smell her sweet, floral fragrance that he picked up hints of when he sat close enough. He couldn't imagine never seeing her again, and he couldn't imagine having to say good-bye.

Reed was in a jam. He didn't want to hurt the woman he loved and was supposed to marry, but he was realizing more than anything, he didn't want to marry Jessica. It broke his heart knowing his truth. How would he tell her, how would he admit that he wasn't ready, and maybe never would be? She wasn't the one. He thought she was, but she wasn't. At first he thought it was cold feet, but he knew it was more than that. It was a girl he barely knew, and every fiber of his being was yelling at him, desperately trying to get his attention. You need to spend more time with that girl.

Reed had no idea what he was going to do. The wedding invitations were due to go out soon enough, and they'd already sent "save the date" cards. Dropping his head to his hands, he realized things were going to get ugly.

This wasn't what he planned, but at this point it was out of his control. His heart wanted what it wanted, and he couldn't go into a marriage when his heart and mind were focused on another woman. How would he tell her? Reed slumped with the weight of the entire world dropping on his shoulders. There was no easy way out of this one.

Sending the text, he felt the rush of adrenaline go through him. "Can I see you tonight? I need to talk to you."

Becky looked at her phone, this was a mistake. She couldn't keep doing this. "I don't think so, I'm sorry." She hated sending those words. She wanted nothing more than to say yes, that she'd see him, spend time with him, be with him, whatever he wanted to hear, but there was no point in going there – they had no future, and dragging this out slowly would be torture.

"Please, I need to see you."

"I have a date," she lied. It made her sick to her stomach, but it was the easiest way out of it. If she didn't seem available, he wouldn't lead her on. It's not like she could have the man, his future was planned, and she didn't belong in it.

"Oh, I see." *Nothing else.* The pit in his stomach wouldn't leave him alone. *A date?* She had a date with somebody. What if she likes him, what if she wants to spend more time with him? Thoughts swirled through his mind, that he might actually lose Becky, when she was never his to begin with.

He swallowed hard and sent another message. "Break your date. He's not the one for you."

Becky did a double take looking at the text. What the…she sent the words before she could stop herself. "Why, who is?"

"Maybe me."

Her heart stopped. Did he just send that? Is this a joke? "You?"

"I don't know."

She hated games. "You're engaged."

"Not after tonight."

She thought she might hyperventilate. Did that say what she thought it said? Her stomach twisted, and she got antsy. Standing up, she paced in circles, *did he just say that?* Looking at her phone again, sure enough the message still said the same thing. Trying to catch her breath, she kept pacing, freaking out quietly inside. She didn't need her co-workers looking over. Her world was about to change, and she wasn't sure what that meant. She knew exactly one thing, Reed was ending his engagement and he wanted to see her.

Finally, catching her breath, she sat back down at her desk and texted, "Tonight, eight o'clock?"

"Let's make it nine. I'm not sure how long this will take."

Becky stared at her phone. This was huge. This was freaking huge. She had to tell Samantha! Wait…not yet. She needed to wait until he broke it off with Jessica first. She didn't want to jump the gun and look like a fool.

Oh my god, oh my god, oh my god. Reed wants me. Me.

Chapter 12

When Reed showed up, he looked grim. "I couldn't do it."

"Oh."

"I'm sorry, Becky. I'm so confused."

"Sure, I can understand. This was probably a mistake for me to show up here tonight." She stood to leave.

"Please don't go," he pleaded. "Just sit and talk to me for a little bit. I need to figure this out."

"You're a grown man, Reed. I think it's obvious I'm attracted to you, but I can't be the other woman you go running to. I'll ask you not to contact me again unless you're single."

"Becky," he called out, but she kept walking. It was the hardest thing she'd ever done.

Reed sat on one of the overstuffed chairs. He blew it. Seeing her, he knew he needed more. It was time to end things with Jessica. He didn't even know how he'd find the words, but he knew it was the right thing to do. He couldn't promise forever to Jessica when all he could think about was Becky.

With a heavy heart, Reed headed home. He'd have to tell her, there was no other way. And even if Becky wasn't the one for him, the idea that another woman lodged herself in his brain told him what he already knew, he couldn't marry Jessica. The drive home was overwhelming. His feelings washed over him, leaving him sad for the end of the relationship that had treated him so well for the last few years.

He'd have to find the words, but how? What would he say? She was going to be angry, sad, and disappointed in him. All the time and effort she'd been planning for their wedding would be for nothing. Reed felt like a jackass and heel. He hated what he was about to do.

It didn't go how he expected, *it went worse*. There were tears, there was yelling, and it got ugly. He never meant to hurt her. He never meant to end things – not like this. He thought they would be together in the end, married, and yet the relief he felt in letting go told him more than he even realized.

He sent a single text later that night. "I'm single."

Becky's jaw dropped. She didn't know what to think. He was single, and that meant he was available, and he wanted her. The twisted knot in her stomach went from joy to panic. He wants to spend time with her. She can't compete with Jessica, she wasn't elegant and graceful. She was awkward and chubby, and oh my gosh, what if they got together, she couldn't get naked in front of the guy, holy shit, what had she gotten herself in to. As the anxiety spread from her toes to the top of her head, Becky's reality sank in. Reed was single and contacting her. He wanted her.

She didn't know what to say, what to text back. She wanted to hear his voice, wanted to talk to him, wanted to text him, but she reigned in her excitement for now. Give him time, his emotions are raw, he just got out of a long term relationship, you aren't over the hurdle. Remorse may set in tomorrow, and he could end up back in Jessica's arms. As much as she wanted to be happy, Becky reserved her feelings for now, for fear they'd get trampled on later.

She had to respond, she couldn't ignore it. He wanted her to know. She had no clue what to say. Afraid she'd ramble and say too much, she simply wrote back, "Okay." She felt like an idiot, she couldn't think of what else to say.

"Can I see you," came back.

"I need time."

He didn't answer. Did she blow it? Shit, here he went and called off his wedding, and all I do is push him away. She wrote back once more, not wanting to sound too eager. "Tomorrow?"

"Tonight?"

Holy shit, she couldn't do tonight, it was already so late. He needs time, they just split up, and he wants to come running over here? This is too soon. He needs time, he needs space.

"Next week?" She wrote back.

"Tomorrow," he suggested
"Tomorrow," she finally agreed.
And so it was decided, she'd see him tomorrow.
Oh my god, oh my god, oh my god. She was going to see him tomorrow.
Texting Sammy, "Are you awake? Need to talk."
Her phone rang seconds later. "What's up?"
"It's Reed. He's single."
"What? Get out of here."
"He just broke up with Jessica. He wants to see me."
"Wow, that's huge."
"Yeah, I can barely breathe. He asked to see me, said he's been thinking about me, and then I went to see him."
"Wait, when?"
"Earlier."
"And you didn't tell me?"
"I was going to, tomorrow."
"What happened?"
"I told him I couldn't see him anymore, because he was engaged."
"And?"
"And he just texted me that he was single and he wants to see me."
"Wow, they've been together forever and were about to get married, Beck."
"Yeah, I know. I've got a lot of mixed feelings. I mean, I'm thrilled for me, but freaked out that he just called off his wedding."
"Yeah, I'm not sure what to think. I mean, I'm happy for you, but he was off limits. That's not cool."

"Wait a minute, do you think I broke them up? I didn't have anything to do with it, this was all him."

"You didn't lead him on or something?"

"Are you serious? Of course not! I can't believe you'd even say that."

"You were really hot for him."

"He's pursuing me, not the other way around." Becky was perturbed at the accusation.

"Okay, I'm just saying, you've been lusting over the guy."

"Privately! Sam, I told him I couldn't see him again, and walked away."

"He obviously wanted to see you if called off his engagement. This is huge."

"You're telling me?"

"Sorry, Becks, it's just big news."

"Huge."

"Forgive me?"

"Of course."

"This is pretty cool. He must really like you."

"So he says. What if now that he can have me, he realizes what he did and doesn't actually want me after all? I'm no Jessica."

"You're so much better than Jessica. You're awesome."

"You're just saying that because I'm your friend."

"I'm saying it because it's true."

"I'm scared."

"What are you afraid of?"

"What if he sees me naked one day and it freaks him out?"

"Slow down, princess. Go on a date first, before you start to think that far ahead."

"You're right, you're right. It's just, have you seen Jessica?"

"I know what you're saying, but Becks, he just dumped her for you."

"Wow." The gravity of it hit her. This was huge. *She was huge*. It was insane thinking that far ahead, but what if when he kissed her he wanted more. She wanted more, but that would mean clothes would be coming off, and she wasn't ready for that. She wasn't ready for his judgment, his disappointment, and his realizing that he'd just ended things with his hot ex Jessica for her fat self.

Her pudge felt pudgier, and without even thinking, she wrapped her arms across her midriff, as if it would shield his eyes from her over abundant curves. He wasn't even here, yet in her mind she knew he'd eventually see her – all of her, and the fog that was deluding his brain into thinking she was something she wasn't would lift, and he'd see her truth. The truth wasn't going anywhere, and suddenly Becky felt sick to her stomach.

The thought of Reed Amwell seeing her naked sent her into a panic, and as her brain spiraled into a pit of self-criticism, she realized maybe she should cancel seeing him after all. It was a mistake; all of this was a mistake. He belongs with Jessica, and no matter how much she wanted to kiss him, to taste his sweet lips, it wasn't supposed to happen. People like Reed didn't happen to girls like Becky.

What felt like a huge win, his wanting to see her, suddenly withered under the weight of the reality. It would turn into regret. He'd realize what he'd done, who he'd chosen, and hate himself. He'd rush back to

Jessica, beg for her forgiveness, and Becky would be left to pick up the pieces of her crumpled heart. *This isn't going to end well.*

"Sam, do you think I should see him? Is this a mistake? It's a mistake isn't it? We don't belong together."

"Wait a minute, something incredible happens and now you're ready to shut it down?"

"I don't know what I want. I mean, I think the guy is hot, but I barely know him."

"Becks, do you like the guy or don't you? Stop overthinking things."

"I'm feeling really overwhelmed. I mean, this is happening. This kind of stuff doesn't happen to me. I'm the kind of girl that gets dumped for someone else. I'm just trying to wrap my head around it all."

"I'm happy for you," Sam sighed. "It could be true love."

"True love? We haven't even gone on a date yet."

"Beck, he broke up with Jessica. He was about to get married. He must be feeling something!"

"I guess," she smiled. "I'm almost afraid to be happy."

"Don't be, it's pretty cool."

"I should sleep, not like I'm going to be able to," Becky said, realizing the time.

"Yeah, I should too. I have an early appointment. I'll talk to you tomorrow, and call me after you talk to Reed. Let me know what happens."

"I will." Hanging up the phone, Becky took a deep breath and broke into a grin. This is real.

Getting through work the following day was going to be damn near impossible. It took forever to fall asleep, and when she finally woke, it was with a smile. Reed broke up with Jessica and wanted to see her – amazing.

The day moved at a snail's pace, and every time she checked the clock, it seemed like only three or four minutes had passed. Her concentration was shot; the only thing she could focus on was what she would say to him, and what he might say to her. She played out possible conversations in her head, trying to think of good responses, but no matter how many times she played the upcoming scenario out, she knew there was no way to predict the outcome.

It was painful sitting there at work, when all she wanted to do was to see Reed. Time was moving in slow motion, and just when she swore time had passed, it was standing still.

As the clock finally ticked toward the close of Becky's working day, she gathered her things and headed out to her car. She could do this, right? Her insecurities were creeping in again, and as much as she wanted to push them away, she couldn't help thinking Reed was making a mistake by choosing her.

What could she offer him? She hated her job, her small business was barely getting off the ground, his ex was five times better looking, and he obviously loved the girl, they were going to get married. Dabbling in the crappy feeling, she pushed it aside and found her strength. *Why can't I be the one he's attracted to? I'm cute, I'm fun, and I'm ambitious.* She tried to convince herself that she was just as much of a catch as Jessica, but it felt like a stretch.

Becky turned her car out of the parking lot and headed home. Distracted in thought, she almost bumped into a car that stopped short. She had to get it together! He was just a guy. Okay, that was a lie; he was unlike any other guy she'd ever known…she had a major crush on an insanely hot guy. And that insanely hot guy wanted to see her.

A quick text conversation set their plans, seven o'clock at her place. She didn't think she could handle this publically. The last thing she needed to worry about was other people. What if he kissed her, would the people around them be judging, wondering why a good looking guy was settling for a fat chick? She hated that she even let stupid thoughts like that cross her mind, but sadly they did.

Becky debated getting another shower, but knew the timing would be cutting it close. She had just enough time to eat something small and touch up her make-up. Should she change her clothes, keep her work clothes on, throw on something more casual? She hated how every tiny decision blew up bigger and bigger, and what should just be a simple conversation was turning into a massive event in her mind.

Standing in front of the mirror, she noticed something she hadn't seen in a while. A huge smile was spread across her face. She liked it.

When her doorbell rang, Becky's heart leapt to her throat. Taking a deep breath, she stood at the door. Calming her nerves the best she was able, she finally answered the door.

He was so handsome. Reed Amwell was the man of her dreams, she was sure of it; she'd seen him there before. He looked like sculpted artwork with his chiseled jaw, broad shoulders, and strong form. Staring into his gorgeous eyes, Becky melted a little inside. His eyes were warm and smiling, and looking right at her. She wanted to stare into them all night long, get lost in her dreams. Locked in place, unable to talk, once again Reed left Becky breathless.

Finally catching herself, she blushed, her cheeks shading crimson and flushing hot. "Hi," she said, barely able to form words. She wanted him so badly that she could taste it.

"Hi," his voice was soft but low.

There was unspoken tension, heated chemistry. There was nothing stopping them anymore.

Stepping back, she allowed him through.

He knew in that instant, he'd made the right decision. He wanted to reach out, he wanted to run his fingers through her hair, pull her close, kiss her, taste her, be with her, and yet he'd only said hello. The look between them said so much more.

Awkwardly, Becky fidgeted with her hands. A finger mindlessly went up to twist a curl in her hair. "Can I get you something to drink?"

"I'm fine, thanks. I was hoping we could talk," he said, sitting on the sofa.

Becky froze. She wanted to sit in his lap. Standing awkwardly, she finally forced herself to move. Exhaling deeply, she sat beside Reed.

Becky bit her lip, sucking it in, her nerves getting the best of her.

"Are you okay?"

"I'm a little nervous," she admitted.

"Nervous?"

"I'm not really sure what's going on. You were engaged last night, and now you're not, and you want to see me, and guys like you don't usually want to see girls like me," she couldn't stop rambling. Her words were like spilled milk, running until somebody could stop them. "And I'm afraid you'll realize it was a mistake, and that you didn't really want to see me after all, and..."

Reed leaned in and kissed her. Her words stopped immediately. He slowly pulled away and looked at Becky. "Relax," he said calmly.

Her fingers went up to her lips, "You kissed me." She said it out of disbelief.

"I'd like to do it again."

Becky stared at him, was this really happening? She nodded slowly.

Reed leaned in, his breath warm, and barely brushing against her lips, he spoke. "I've wanted to kiss you for a while."

Becky closed her eyes, and as he moved the slightest bit closer, he parted his lips and met hers. Time stood still, and as she felt his mouth on hers, Becky swore she might drop dead in that very instant. It was the single best moment of her life, and as he kissed her sweetly, his lips soft and most importantly against hers, she sighed, literally sighed into his mouth.

This must be what heaven is like, she thought. It had to be, because there was no other way to describe the magic she was feeling. As Reed kissed her, Becky's brain swirled with a rainbow of colors. Slowly he lifted his hand to her hair, and raked his fingers through her soft blonde curls. Her hair was like silk, and gripping the back of her head gently, he pulled her closer.

Reed's kiss got hungrier, more passionate, and just as he suspected kissing Becky Holgate was everything he hoped it would be.

Becky's mind was exploding, and with every second that passed, she expected it to stop, just end, be over, and for Reed to jump up and realize it was a mistake. She wanted to enjoy it without the thoughts rushing through her brain, but they wouldn't stop. She was in a war with her own mind.

Reed leaned her back and pressed into her, as if he couldn't get enough. *Oh shit, this was truly happening.*

Pulling back just for a second, Reed looked at Becky, and then went back in for another kiss. Stunned but elated, Becky greedily accepted every single kiss he offered. Finally relaxing into the moment, she reached up and ran her fingers through his dark hair. Her fires were burning, and with every minute that passed, she shed the shyness she wore. She wanted Reed; the moisture between her legs told her what she already knew.

As their kisses slowed, Reed smiled. "I desperately wanted to kiss you the other night at the coffee shop," was all he said. He would have said more, but his lips were back on Becky's.

"Wow," Becky whispered, as they came up for air.

Reed pulled back and stood, "I'm sorry."

"Sorry? Where did that come from?" Becky was confused. One second he was practically on top of her, and the next he was apologizing.

"I threw myself on you. I should have given you some space. I'm not really sure what's going on," he said, now pacing. "I'm drawn to you like a bee to honey, and yet I'm just out of a relationship. The idea that you had a date and somebody else might step in before I could kind of freaked me out."

Becky watched the man teeter between assertion and confusion. "Reed, are you sure you want to be here?"

"Very sure," he said looking at her. "Why, do you question that?"

"It's just that you only called off your engagement last night, and yet here you are in my living room today. Don't you need time to heal? Time to make sure you're doing the right thing?"

"I am doing the right thing."

"You walked away from a long term relationship on a whim. What if you regret your decision?"

"I can't stop thinking about you," he sighed.

"You barely know me."

Reed dropped his head. "I don't know what I want." He sat back down. "It all happened so fast. I thought I was getting married, and then you walked in, and it's like a fog lifted. Suddenly my world had color again."

Becky smiled hearing his description, but she knew he wasn't ready to jump from one relationship to another. He needed to be sure. "I think you need to absorb what happened still. If this is what you want after you've taken time to heal from your break up, I'll be here with open arms, but to just jump so quickly, quite honestly it concerns me. Don't get me wrong, I want nothing more than for you to kiss me again," she said softly, "but I don't think you're ready for this."

Reed looked at Becky. He hated how impulsive he felt, when she was all calm and logical. His insides were melting like heated butter, but she had a point. It all happened so fast. He needed time; time to figure out exactly what he wanted.

"I should go," he said quietly.

"I wish you'd stay, just for a little while."

Reed nodded and sat down. "I feel like a fool."

"You? Why? Oh my gosh, you made my day," she gushed.

"I did?"

"If you haven't noticed, I have a massive crush on you, but I just don't want you to jump into something before you're ready."

It was intense, there were emotions flying, and neither knew what to do.

A loud crash from the bedroom had Becky groaning. "Bad kitty," she yelled out. "Excuse me," she said turning toward Reed. "I'll be right back. I need to see what Bella destroyed this time."

She found Bella sitting on her bed, all innocent, licking her paw. "What did you do?" She walked around the bed, and saw her alarm clock tossed on the floor. *That damn cat.*

Reed was leaning on the doorframe to her bedroom. "Is everything okay?"

She nodded slowly. "Just the cat," she said softly. He looked so hot, all masculine and muscled, and so freaking handsome. Becky stopped talking.

Walking over, Reed reached out and pulled her into his arms. Looking down, he tipped her chin up and kissed her.

She could barely breathe. Becky was in trouble. She was falling fast, and if he kept kissing her like this, she'd lose any sense she had left.

Pulling back, Becky sighed, "We need to talk." She hated, absolutely hated that her sensible side was kicking in. She wanted this, wanted him, but was terrified he wasn't thinking things through. Barely any time had elapsed, and he was kicking into high gear. They needed time and space, and he needed to make sure he was heading in the right direction.

Reed arched an eyebrow, "About?"

"I hate myself for saying this," she started, but he dotted her lips with kisses and then left a trail across her jaw, and down along her neck.

"Then don't," he got out between tiny nibbles.

"Reed, you're moving too fast. It feels so good, but you're not ready for this."

"Shhh," he whispered, nuzzling into her, milking her skin with his lips.

Becky's entire body tingled. Tilting her head to the side, she let him continue. All thoughts, any common sense left her mind, and the only thing she could focus on was the insanely attractive man nibbling on her neck.

Inhaling deeply, she picked up on hints of his cologne, masculine and woodsy. She wanted nothing more than for him to make sweet love to her. Becky closed her eyes, sinking deeper and deeper into the sensations Reed was offering. Her knees went weak, and as her heart bounced around, all full of pitter patter, she finally let go.

Reed's hands slid down her back, resting on the curve of her bottom, and with a small groan, he squeezed her gently.

Finally coming up for air, Reed smiled at Becky. "Maybe we could go out on a date sometime?"

"I'd like that," she answered breathlessly.

Chapter 13

Saying good-bye, Becky felt all gooey inside. She wanted to pinch herself to make sure she wasn't dreaming. He was really here, and a great kisser, and wow when he squeezed her ass and groaned she about died.

Closing the door behind him, she thought about his mouth on hers, his hands running through her hair, and his delicious aroma. She practically floated to the sofa, and sinking into it, she closed her eyes, this time remembering his lips on her neck, nibbling, nuzzling, and suckling her skin.

Drifting on the high of the evening, Becky realized if she died right now, right here on this spot, she'd die a happy woman. Reed Amwell had not only left his fiancée to be with her, but he showed up on her doorstep the very next day.

With the weekend coming, Becky planned to focus on her business. Reed would be unavailable as he'd be helping Jessica move out. She was moving in with a friend for now, and as difficult as it was, he offered his truck and himself to make the move go as smoothly as possible.

It was still incredibly painful for her, but when it came down to it, Jessica had an ulterior motive. He'd certainly change his mind if he was involved in the move. The reality of her leaving, it would hit him, and he'd ask her to stay telling her it was all a mistake.

Jessica could have asked other people to help her move, but by having him there, she hoped he'd come to his senses. She knew he still loved her. She didn't know what was going on with him, but she was convinced it was cold feet. You don't just throw away a relationship like this without a reason. They weren't over yet, she was sure of it.

As hurt and angry as she was the other day, she refused to let go. Reed was her life. It's not like he even found out about Matthew, not that it mattered, she had ended this with him months ago. Sure she had a tiny affair, but when Reed finally came around and proposed after what felt like forever, she knew he was committed. That was all it took to end things with Matthew.

It's not like she loved the guy, it was purely for the sex anyway. Matthew was a co-worker that filled a need. She wasn't attached to the guy, but for a while, he offered her the thrill that she needed. Frustrated after years of dating Reed, and his refusal to take their relationship to the next step, she couldn't help but stray. Now that it was all behind her, they could move forward. Maybe that's all this was, maybe he had an itch, or cold feet, or whatever. She'd soothe things over, and remind him why they belonged together.

On moving day, Jessica showed up bright and early, only she left her friend at home. Opening the door, Reed looked confused. "I thought Gina was coming to help you."

"I thought we should talk first," she said walking in. Slowly stripping off her shirt, she turned around to reveal the lace teddy beneath her clothing.

Reed shut her down before she could start. "Don't."

"This is a mistake," she pleaded her case. "Reed, baby, you love me."

"I do love you, Jess, but I'm not in love with you. It's time for us to go our separate ways."

Pulling her shirt back over her head, she was furious. "I'll send for my things," she spat out, walking out the door. The pain she felt ripped her to shreds, and as Jessica left her shattered heart on the floor, Reed closed the door behind her.

Sitting, Reed's heart felt heavy. He didn't want it to end this way, but he knew it was what he had to do. The least he could do was start sorting through some stuff. He wanted nothing more than to put it off, go for a run, or find a healthy distraction, but the work had to get done.

There was so much to do. Jessica had pulled a lot of her clothes and shoes, but they still had to sort through their home office, the kitchen, and decide what was what. He missed Bean, but she made it clear that there was no way she'd be able to exist without him. He'd gotten attached to the little dog, but knew he was her baby. After breaking her heart, he couldn't fight for Bean too. The house felt empty and quiet. Without Jess here, or Bean wondering about, he wondered what it would be like to live alone again. It had been such a long time since he was alone – and here he was ready to jump into another relationship.

Maybe it was a mistake. Maybe he should slow down, take some time, but there was something about Becky Holgate that drew him in. He wanted to be around her, and yet how could he offer himself fully if he was still getting over this past relationship. The more he thought about the details, the more they overwhelmed him. That run sounded like a good idea, and clearing his head was the only thing he could muster right now.

Covered in sweat after a good run, Reed climbed into the shower. He should call Becky and see if she's free. Maybe they could go out. There he went again, jumping in without taking time to breathe. On second thought, get the work done around the house. He'd sort through the files in the home office and separate their stuff. It was tedious work, but it wouldn't do itself.

It was in the third file drawer. Going through stacks of paper, he found the card haphazardly shoved underneath. He didn't recognize it. Picking it up, he opened it with curiosity. He felt ill seeing the note written inside, with a date drawn in a heart. Who the fuck was Matthew, and why was it dated during their relationship?

Reed got up and pushed the file cabinet over in disgust. No words could take away the pain he was feeling. She cheated on him, and no amount of denial could take away the words he saw. Everything inside of him bunched up. Wanting to slam a hole through the wall, he stopped himself and started pacing. How could she have done this to him? They were getting married. He was a fool to believe she'd been faithful all this time. Reed crumpled into the office chair and dropped his head into his hands as the hot tears fell. How long had it gone on, and was she going to run into his arms?

He felt like a fool. All this time he thought he was the only one. *Fuck her*.

Becky sat reading the tutorial, trying to figure out how to make a website. She might have to rely on one of those quickie cheap sites that were like clunky building blocks. At least she'd have a presence. Now that she had a couple of people, she needed to work on her professional angle. How could they take her seriously as a business owner, if she couldn't even make a website? She'd eventually have to pay somebody, but it's not like she had a lot of money to work with.

Flipping through other dating websites, she felt overwhelmed. What was she thinking, trying to get this business off the ground? It was silly to believe she could do it all by herself. Feeling defeated, Becky gave up in that moment, but only for a second. *No, you need to start somewhere, so just start from square one. You can do this.*

Looking at the applications, she made some calls, trying to set up her first date. She had two guys, and she had to at least try. How else would she reach her dream if she didn't start somewhere? Becky felt better after talking to one of the girls, telling her about a potential date match. The woman was excited, and said yes to the guy Becky had proposed. Now she had to call him and make the match. They could meet at an agreed upon location, keeping it public for the first date. Becky asked the girl if she could have the guy email her, and then contacted him.

She squealed hanging up the phone. They would email each other to set their meet-up. She'd done it; she hooked up her first two people. They both liked outdoor activities, and had a love of nature. It was a start! Okay, now to figure out this stupid website. Maybe Reed could help her after all. She hated to ask, but he had offered before. She didn't want to bother him, since he was helping Jessica move out today. The thought of them alone together made her nervous. Her worst fear was that he'd realize what a mistake it was and want Jessica back.

Becky was torn between wanting to give him time to deal with the split, and being afraid if she waited too long he'd change his mind about her. When he kissed her, wow, and all she wanted was the chance to kiss him again. Becky got lost remembering their kiss again. Closing her eyes, she pictured him in front of her.

Sheepishly grinning, she went to her nightstand and pulled out a vibrator. With a daydream and an image of Reed, Becky took matters into her own hands, sinking back into the sofa, remembering that kiss and him nuzzling into her neck.

Relaxed and breathing ragged after an orgasm, Becky smiled and went back to her desk. She'd figure out this website once and for all. Buried in tutorials, she was finally making the tiniest bit of leeway when the doorbell rang.

Standing, her brain still wrapped around details of the tutorial instructions, she opened the door. Reed was the last person she expected to see. Only, he didn't look at her dreamily, he looked like a crushed little boy.

"Are you okay?" She opened the door wider, inviting him in.

"Yeah, I mean, I guess."

"What happened?"

"Just something with Jess," he said, his voice hurting.

Here it comes; he's going to tell her he got back together with Jessica. Becky braced herself for the news.

"Anyway, it's over. There's no going back."

Becky didn't know whether to be relieved or feel bad for the guy. He looked broken. "Can I ask?"

"I'm not ready to talk about it."

"I understand," she said following him into the living room. "Can I offer you a beer?"

It was in that moment that she saw the pink vibrator standing proud and at attention on her coffee table. Reed must have seen it at the same time. In slow motion he turned around and grinned. Becky panicked and ran for the table.

Reed reached it before she did and picked up the sex toy, holding it up. "What have we here? Have you been participating in extra-curricular activities?" His voice teased, and she wanted to fade into the walls, blending in unseen.

Becky's eyes opened wide, and as she turned fifteen shades of red, she started babbling nonsense. "That's not mine, I mean, it's mine, it's umm, not what it looks like, okay, it's totally what it looks like, holy shit I'm horrified. I didn't think, I mean, I didn't expect you, oh my gosh, I'm going to die of embarrassment. God, strike me down now."

The corners of his mouth turned up, smiling at her attempt to squirm out of the predicament. She was so cute. "What is it? I wonder what this button does," he said turning it on. Laughing, he watched as the tip rotated and the base vibrated. "Oh Becky, you naughty girl," he teased.

The whirring of the battery stunned her. She stood frozen like a deer caught in headlights. Finally snapping out of the horror, Becky went to grab it from him, to hide the evidence, but he raised his arm up, holding it out of her reach.

"Reed, give that to me!"

"Becky, Becky, Becky…does your mother know about this?" He said mockingly, and added a few "tsk,

tsk, tsk" sounds to hammer home the effect of complete humiliation.

"She'd die, like I'm dying of embarrassment right now," Becky clamored, trying to get the sex toy from the man in her living room.

Lowering his arm, he brought it to his face and inhaled. If she could have died on the spot, she would have. "Very nice," he whispered. He finally lowered his arm and gave it to her. "Here you go," he smiled.

Becky looked down and quickly ran to her bedroom, shoving it in her nightstand drawer. She'd never live this one down. She'd never been so mortified in her life. Okay, there was one time when her pants fell down during college, when her elastic band snapped in her slacks, and right there in the middle of the campus down they went, but this easily ranked as the second most embarrassing moment of her life. Okay, wait, that's not true, maybe the third or fourth most embarrassing, but it was up there.

Reed sat down, "I think Jess was cheating on me," he said quietly.

"What?" Becky was stunned. Who would cheat on someone like him?

"I found something while I was cleaning up. Anyway, I'm feeling kind of heartbroken."

"I can imagine."

"I'm sorry; I shouldn't be talking about this with you."

"Reed, I don't know what this is going on between us, but above anything I'm your friend. If you need to talk, then talk."

"You're something special." Reed squeezed her hand.

She wanted to smother him in kisses, but the timing obviously wasn't appropriate. Lightening the mood, "Do you want to go get something to eat?"

"Yeah, actually that sounds good," he said standing.

What had started out as a crappy day was turning into a better one. He realized he'd need time to heal, time to get over the relationship he was getting out of, but he hoped Becky would wait for him. He wanted to spend more time with her, but he didn't want to jump in too fast. He'd been with Jessica for a long time, and he'd feel the sting for a while.

After lunch out, Reed headed home to finish the job he'd started earlier. With a simple, small peck on the cheek, he thanked Becky for cheering him up. He couldn't make promises, but if she was willing to stick around, he'd like to get to know her better. Becky smiled, telling him he was worth the wait.

On heading home, Becky thought about the turn of events. Here Reed thought he was the bad guy, when Jess had already been cheating on him. It was hard to see him hurting, but she was selfishly grateful that he wasn't getting back together with the stunning woman.

Calling Sam, she relayed the news of the day.

"You're kidding? She cheated on him? She always sounded so in love with the guy."

"I don't know all the details, just what he found."

"Wow."

"Yeah, and guess what else he found?"

"What?"

"He saw my vibrator sitting out on the table!"

"Why was your vibrator...oh."

"Yeah, figure it out. Anyway, I wasn't expecting him to come over, and just forgot about it."

"I'd die," she started.

"I nearly did. I was so embarrassed. It happened in slow motion. I look over, see it sitting there and realize he's seen it. I go to dive for it, but it's too late, he's picked it up. He picked the damn thing up!"

"Oh my god, then what happened? What did he say?"

"He starts teasing me, and he's waving it up over his head, out of my reach. I was dying, totally humiliated."

"What did you do?"

"I'm freaking out, going "give me that", and I'm sure I was twenty shades of red, but he was having a grand old time. So then, he goes and slides it under his nose, and sniffs it. I have never been so mortified in my life…" she started.

"What about the time your pants fell down."

"Yeah whatever, just let me tell you the damn story."

"Go on," Samantha laughed.

"So, he slides it under his nose, and smells it right in front of me. I'm cringing inside, and he goes, "very nice" and I'm dying, dying I tell you. He finally hands it back to me, and I ran and shoved it into my drawer."

"You should have asked him to use it on you," she snorted, "since you were probably thinking about him when you used it earlier."

"Stop!" Becky was trying not to laugh, but it was funny. She could laugh now even though earlier she was horrified.

"Hey Reed," she mocked in a silly voice, "Could you show me how to use this? I'm not sure I'm doing it right."

"Oh my god, you're a freak."

"Hey baby, how about you…"

"Okay, that's enough," Becky said, shutting her down. "No more."

"Fine, you're no fun," Sam teased. "I'll stop being a *dick*."

"Ha ha, you're funny. Oh, that's right, you're not."

"So what do you think he's going to do? It sounds like he's pretty interested."

"I know, but I'm afraid he's rebounding, you know. Like he's hurting, and here I am."

"That's not entirely true. He was interested in you before he split with her."

"I guess, it just seems too soon, like he's moving too fast. I like the guy, but I don't want to be a passing fancy."

"Yeah, I totally get that. I don't know what to tell you, Becks. I just think if a hot guy landed in my lap, I wouldn't walk away or let go too easily."

"Unless he has a weird laugh?"

"Okay, this is not about me. What's your point?"

"I don't have one. Oh wait, yes I do," she mocked sarcastically. "You're great at doling out advice, just not taking it."

"Becks, he laughed like a girl. I couldn't live with that. Besides, it frees him up for your dating agency."

"I forgot to tell you, I hooked up my first couple!"

"No way, when are they going out?"

"I'm not sure, they're going to email each other and set something up. I told them each to get back to me so I can see how it went. Did they like the match and stuff, so I can use the information for future dates."

"Nice, do you think they will?"

"I hope so," she sighed. "I think I just pictured this different. In my brain, my business was working and full of people, but this starting up and only having a few people, and silly details I overlooked is so much harder than I thought it would be."

"You'll get there," Sam commiserated. "It's tough. It took a long time for me to grow my client list. Now I have to worry about Pristine Pooches stealing my clients."

"Don't you guys have an agreement?"

"Sure, but we slept together, and we went our separate ways, it's not like he owes me anything. I'm hoping he sticks to his word. It's not like I can hold anything over his head. Anyway, you'll get there. You should host a small event and try to get more people interested. And when your website is up and working, that will get attention too."

"I hope so," she sighed. "It's taking forever."

Chapter 14

Samantha poured the wine as Becky grabbed the snacks, tossing them on the coffee table. Grabbing a pen and paper, the girls were ready to brainstorm. Deciding to throw a singles dance, it was time to figure out how to advertise the event.

"Okay, so Art said you can use the banquet room at his place. We've got space, now we need people."

"Right, I'll need your help setting it up, and deciding how to decorate so it has a theme or something. I was thinking if we dropped by the barbeque place, we could pass out flyers on Poker night, there might be some guys there."

"Hey, what about Pete's Pub? It's the watering hole for ball games. Baseball goes week long, maybe you could find some guys there."

"Will you help," Becky asked sweetly, knowing she would freeze up on talking to everyone and passing out flyers. "What should they say? Should I advertise it as a simple singles dance, or should I clarify I'm looking for clients, and that it's for a plus size dating agency?"

"That's tough. I'd say the more people you get there the better. While you're there, you could approach people individually, or put out applications people could fill. Better yet, if your website is ready, you could have it posted all over, so people could check it out."

"Yeah," Becky sighed, "I'm still working on that."

"Ask Reed to do it. Didn't you say he volunteered when you first met him anyway?"

"I just feel weird asking."

"Do you want to be stuck in your job forever? You need to get this off the ground, or your business is going to flop before it can succeed."

"You're right…what? What are you doing?" Becky stared at Sam as she dug at her shirt.

Shifting, moving, turning, twisting, her fingers prying, "Damn underwire bra is digging in. I think the wire broke through the fabric, and it's poking me."

"I wish they'd perfect these things all ready. Did I tell you I paid forty bucks for one, and the stupid wire pushed through the corner in a couple of weeks? What is that? I swear I'm going back to non-wired soon."

"I tried skipping the underwire, my boobs were flat like pancakes," she sighed. "Stupid bra," she grunted, pulling and trying to wedge the wire back into place. "I mean, they're fine for a bit, but then you lose shape through the day, and they just look deflated. It was sad really. I just don't think I should have to suffer like this to keep my girls up."

"Better now?" She saw her friend settle back into the sofa.

"For now, until the damn wire makes an escape again. Why is it so difficult to make a bra?"

"I hear you. Oh, did I tell you I got a lingerie catalog in the mail? You know, from the big name company. I don't know why I paged through it, it was torture. I mean, you know they don't carry my size, but I still felt the need to flip through it. Talk about feeling lumpy. I was so depressed. If I had a body like that, I'd walk around naked all the time."

"You would not," she laughed. "You say you would, but you wouldn't. You'd be too shy. I would walk around naked, but you'd at least need a bikini on."

"You think? I could totally walk around naked if I looked like that. I'd strut right down the street."

"You're such a liar. I'd be all, let's go strut naked, and you'd be like, let me put something on first."

Becky shook her head. "Fine, I'll admit it, maybe I'd need to wear a leopard spotted bikini or something, and I'd totally slide on heels to make my legs longer, but I could do it like that."

"I knew you couldn't do it naked. You want to believe you could do it naked, but you're not a naked kind of girl."

"You are."

"Oh, I totally am. You'd have to hold me back. I figure there's probably a reason I'm chubby. It's to save the world from my strutting around naked constantly," Sam gloated.

"Could you imagine? I'd be getting calls from the police department, asking me to pick up my naked friend that they picked up again. We found her in the produce aisle, can you tell your friend to put clothes on. Of course I'd have to say, I've tried, but she's got an amazing body, so she doesn't believe in clothes anymore." Becky thought on it, and then asked, "Do you think girls with great bodies think about walking around naked?"

"I don't know, maybe they don't appreciate it, since they've always had it. On the other hand, maybe they're really attention whores, but are afraid society would shun them. They aren't risk takers obviously, because how often do you see it happen?"

"You're a risk taker," Becky added.

"A total risk taker, I'd do it."

"I bet you would. Anyway, what should the flyers say?"

"Naked women, guys would show up."

"You're a big help. Okay, back to work…"

The girls tossed some more ideas around, and by the end of the night Becky had a plan. They'd throw a single's dance to try to drum up more business. They had a list of places she could pass out flyers, and they'd keep the décor simple. Advertising the dance, she could put an ad in the small local paper, and maybe even get them to write about it. She'd call and see if they'd be willing to feature her singles dance in their upcoming events section. Becky smiled, feeling the plan come together. Now she just needed to figure out the website. Reed was her best option, but she figured for now she'd put up a cheap building block website until she had something better.

With another bottle of wine gone, and a full list of ideas, Becky felt it was a productive night.

Sam was feeling sappy by the end of the bottle. "I was thinking of calling Wyatt. What do you think?"

"Wyatt? Seriously, why would you even give that guy a second of thought? Sammy, it's the wine talking. He's not good for you."

"He has a massive penis."

"No, he's a massive dickhead."

"Big dick," she used her hands to add emphasis.

"No booty calls. You only end up hurt."

"Becks, why is he such a jerk?"

"I don't know. Don't call him, you always regret it."

"Yeah, I know. It's just sometimes I want to spend time with him. I really liked the guy."

"He treated you like crap. When you gained weight, he was a dick about it."

She nodded, "I hate how he changed."

"He didn't change, your body did. His asshole side just came out."

"It was my fault really; I got lazy about taking care of myself."

"Don't you dare make excuses for him. The things he said to you were uncalled for."

"I loved him, Becks."

Becky's tone softened. "You deserve better, Sam. I know you cared about the guy, but he was horrible for your self-esteem. He was cruel, and you deserve so much more."

Sam nodded in agreement. "I thought he was the one."

"I know, babe. But one day you'll meet the real Mr. Right, and he'll love you as you are, no matter what."

"I hope so."

"You will."

"What about Reed, when are you going to see him next?"

"Probably this week, but I feel weird with everything going on. He's obviously going to need time to get over this stuff with Jessica, but I'm afraid if I give him too much time, he'll lose interest."

"It will all work out."

"I hope so. I like the guy. I feel comfortable around him, and he's a great kisser," she smiled softly.

"You know who was a great kisser? Wyatt."

"Stop, don't go there. Besides, maybe you'll meet somebody at the single's dance."

"Maybe Wyatt will show up."

"Sam, let it go. He was mean. We don't want mean guys in our lives."

"You're right, you're right. We deserve better. Why do I do this to myself? No booty call, I promise."

"Good girl."

The phone rang later that night… "I was weak. I called."

"Oh, Sam."

"It's okay, he blew me off."

"I'm sorry, hon."

"Don't be. I felt like a whore, but when I hung up after he said no, I got angry. I think angry works for me. It's better than feeling lonely and pathetic."

"You're not pathetic."

"I know, I'm angry now, so I'm past that feeling."

"You'll find the right guy someday."

"I wish he'd hurry up and get here. I miss him already."

Chapter 15

With a nice mention in the local paper, the event got more notice than Becky expected. She was thrilled when over thirty people showed. Sam found a local DJ to host the party and bartered the price down. The DJ had three dogs, and with an exchange in services, she was able to finagle a half price deal.

Grateful the event wasn't costing too much, Becky went about setting things up. When Reed showed up, she couldn't stop smiling. She hadn't seen him much of the past few weeks, as he was sorting through his life after the break-up. They stayed in touch, talking constantly via text and email, but Becky was trying to give him space. He promised he was interested and wasn't going anywhere, but he needed a little bit of time to work through some feelings.

Walking into the room, Reed caught sight of Becky. She was glowing, bouncing around setting things up. On turning around, Becky's smile told him what he needed to know. She was thrilled to see him.

"You made it," her voice was warm.

"I wouldn't miss the chance to dance with you."

Leaning up, Becky kissed Reed's cheek. "You're sweet. I have a few more things to do over here, but people should be arriving soon."

"Sounds good, how can I help?"

As the night went on, more and more people showed up. What started out slow, ended with a room full of people. It wasn't a huge turn-out, but it was a lot more people than she anticipated. Becky was nervous the room would look sparse, but with well over thirty people, it was filling in. The DJ did his part getting people dancing, and as the night wore on, Becky made her rounds, talking about her business, pointing people to a table with applications.

Watching Becky work the room made Reed smile. He finally caught her hand as she was walking by. "Can I have this dance?"

Becky blushed. "I'd like that."

As the music slowed, Reed placed his hand on Becky's lower back, pulling her into him. With his other, he placed it on her shoulder, letting his fingers move to her hair. Stroking through her hair gently, he placed her head onto his chest and held the girl close.

Time stood still. Standing in Reed's arms, her head on his chest, Becky realized she was in heaven. This had to be what heaven felt like, she was sure of it.

Pressed to Reed, the music playing a slow sway, Becky moved with Reed. With each breath he took, she felt his chest rise. Being so close, his woodsy cologne filled her senses. She could hear his heart beating, and it was as if every single beat was for her.

Holding her close, Reed let his fingers play in her hair. It was soft and silky, and the prettiest shade of blonde he'd ever seen. It was like a golden halo she wore, highlighting her milky complexion. Becky tipped her head, looking up to him, and in that moment he couldn't help himself. Lowering his head, he kissed her sweet lips.

There was an unspoken connection between them. Staring into his eyes, she saw desire. Everything inside of her wanted to leave the dance, to take Reed home with her and make love to him, but she knew she couldn't leave. This was her event, and even though her world was simply the man before her, she knew this wasn't their moment. It was certainly a moment, but it wasn't time for *that* yet.

When the song ended, she didn't want to part from him. He made it difficult, whispering intimate and sexy things in her ear, his hot breath making her damp between her legs. She wanted him, desperately wanted him, but she'd have to wait.

The looks bouncing between then through the evening had Becky wanting to rush the night, and get this event over with. Business could wait; she was hungry for personal pleasure. Oblivious to anything but Reed, she didn't see Samantha connecting to somebody new. She should have seen it, the way Sam was smiling. Only Becky couldn't see anything but Reed from that moment on.

Reed reached out and took Becky's hand, as she walked by, checking on things. Stopping her in her tracks, he pulled her close once again. "Take me home tonight," he whispered.

Her heart raced. Were they ready? She thought they were, but maybe they should wait. She knew there was no way they were waiting. The tension and chemistry between them was sizzling, and just with a look, she was ready to strip down to her panties. Reed had that kind of effect on her.

Bringing her hand to his mouth, he kissed her tenderly, and then took a finger into his mouth, sucking it while looking at her. "You and me," was all he said. He didn't need to say anything else. "Save me another dance," he smiled, as she finally pulled away. She had to; she had to keep her senses. If she stood here any longer, she'd forget she was the host of the event. She only had eyes for Reed, but she had to wrap up this party.

Her heart racing, she made one last final round before the dance started to wind down. She made sure people took applications with them, and asked them to consider her services. As the final stragglers made their way out, she was left with Reed. Sam smiled and whispered she met somebody, and then headed out to say goodnight to her new interest.

As the room cleared and things were cleaned up, the adrenaline of the event was wearing down. All that was left was space between Becky and Reed. She wanted to close that gap, she wanted to take him home, she wanted to make love to him, and she was sure he wanted that too.

"Do you want to come over," she whispered to the man before her.

"If I come over tonight, I won't leave until tomorrow."

Becky nodded, understanding what he was saying. "Follow me home."

Reed smiled.

Becky gripped her steering wheel, realizing what was happening. When she got home, when they went inside, they would make love. They both knew, both felt the connection, and as she drove her heart beat faster than she thought possible.

Pulling into her driveway, she took a deep breath as Reed pulled in behind her. This was really going to happen. Getting out of her car and walking with Reed, they went inside, Becky knowing her life was about to change.

The tension was thick, and before Becky's insecurities could surface, she saw her cat suspended from the curtains. "Bella, get down!"

The cat had clawed its way up her drapes and now clung precariously close to the top. On seeing Becky the cat shot off the curtains, splayed out like a flying squirrel. Landing on the sofa below, crack kitty flew across the floor in a wild pattern of zigs and zags.

"What the…?" Reed laughed, watching the cat run in a mad dash around the living room.

Becky groaned, "She does this after, umm, after she relieves herself." She sighed on seeing pulls in the curtain fabric. She needed to declaw this cat before it destroyed her home.

"What? You're kidding right?"

"I wish," Becky sighed. "She acts like using the litter box is some miraculous thing, and when she leaves me little surprises in there, she goes tearing around here like she owns the place."

"That's some cat."

"You're telling me."

"I wish I felt like that after using the bathroom. Imagine how cool that would be."

Becky laughed, "You're a goof."

As the cat mellowed out, Becky realized how much tension was broken. She didn't know if it was a good thing or a bad thing. On entering her home, all she wanted was to tear off his clothes and climb into bed with him, but now she was having second thoughts. Maybe they should slow things down.

"Reed, about tonight," she started.

"Having second thoughts?"

"I don't know," she hesitated. "It's not that I don't want to be with you, it's just that I want you to be ready to move forward."

"I understand."

"I'm afraid to get attached to you, and I will get attached if we do this," she warned.

Reed moved in for an embrace, "I want you to get attached," he said quietly.

Becky smiled.

"You gave me space, but I want to close that gap," he said leaning down to kiss Becky's forehead.

Reed looked at the full figured girl; he'd never been drawn to women like Becky before. He usually found himself drawn to girls with long racehorse legs, slender waists, and a smaller frame. Only there was something primal in him, and her soft curves had him hungry to see more. She was rounder, fuller, and more voluptuous than other women he'd been with.

Reed wanted to take her in, admire her soft flesh, and feel her body pressed to his. There was something raw and beautiful about Becky, something that spoke to him in ways he wasn't expecting. Her full hips, her breasts, there was a lushness that he wanted to explore, and his hard cock told him all he needed to know. He was insanely attracted to the woman before him.

Becky felt Reed's eyes on her, and for a moment she felt beautiful. She wanted nothing more than to make love to the man holding her; only tiny seeds of insecurity were popping up, forcing her to look at something she didn't want to. Feeling self-conscious of her body, she caught herself sucking her stomach in out of habit.

Would he still be attracted to her when she was naked? She made a mental note to keep the lights off and hide under the covers. At least her flesh would be less obvious. She couldn't know he wanted to celebrate her flesh, and that her soft, lush curves made him want her even more. How could she when she was her biggest critic, always feeling less worthy because she'd gained more weight than she'd like.

Reed's kiss pulled her out of her thoughts, drowning her in nothing but passion and lust. Pulling back, she took in the handsome man holding her, his dark hair, his dark eyes, and the way he was looking at her made her weak in the knees. And he smelled so good, she wanted to just sniff him over and over, but she knew he'd think she was weird, but holy cow, his cologne did something to her.

It felt like a dream. Guys like Reed didn't usually go for girls like Becky.

The room suddenly felt quiet, and pulling out of his arms for just a moment, she told him she wanted to put on some music. The silence echoed and her thoughts swirled. Finding a nice mix, she let the music spill from the speakers, just loud enough to offer atmosphere.

Reed was behind her, his hands on her shoulders, caressing, squeezing, touching her. His drive was out of his control at this point; he needed to hold her, feel her, and pulled her back into his arms. "Dance with me," he finally whispered only inches from her face.

Becky turned around and looked up at her soon to be lover. Falling into his arms, they swayed quietly together, bodies pressed tightly, feeling the weight of the moment. The chemistry between them was on fire, and as they stood in each other's arms, Reed knew it was time.

The look between them said more than words could. Reaching down, he took Becky's hand and led her to the bedroom. As Becky followed, her heart beat harder and faster, racing like crazy. This was really going to happen.

Standing near the bed, Reed cupped Becky's face in his hands. Leaning in to kiss her, he quietly asked if she was sure she wanted to do this. Becky nodded, looking up to Reed.

No words were spoken, and for a moment as their gaze was locked, it felt like they were the only people in the world. Lowering his head, Reed enveloped Becky in a passionately heated kiss, leaving her breathless. Feeling his hardness pressed against her hip, she was grateful he found her attractive. She prayed that his erection wouldn't wilt on seeing her naked. There was only one way to find out.

Reed slowly unbuttoned Becky's shirt, one pearl button at a time. Becky's heart was about to leap out of her chest, as her nerves were shaking and her breathing got more ragged. Reaching the final button, he moved his hands to her shoulders, reaching underneath and slowly helping her shed the fabric covering her body.

Becky looked at Reed, wondering what he was thinking, and felt vulnerable.

"You're beautiful," he said quietly, as his mouth moved to her shoulder. Nibbling and kissing her, his mouth moved toward her neck.

Closing her eyes, Becky sank into the sensation of his lips milking her skin. Everything inside of her tingled, and as he moved to the curve of her neck, directly below her hairline, electricity shot through her. Arching her back, unable to control her body's movement, she knew she'd be putty in his hands.

As his lips tended to her neck, his fingers were working to undo her bra. Unhooking the material, he slid the bra down and off. Her round, full breasts were exposed, and drew the attention of his large, masculine hands.

Gently squeezing her, his fingers drew down across her breasts, stopping at a nipple. Gently he rolled it between his thumb and forefinger, teasing her with a soft pinch, and then rolling it again. His mouth never left her neck, but was slowly moving lower to meet his fingers.

Dotting tender kisses down across her chest, and then at her cleavage, he focused his attention on her other nipple. His warm mouth encased her breast, suckling in her nipple, and with just the right amount of pressure, had her moaning quietly. Becky rolled her head back, feeling his lips on her, and all she wanted was for him to never stop, to never leave her side, and to pleasure her until the morning light.

"You're breasts are amazing," he whispered, leaving her heart fluttering.

"Thank you," she barely got out. Talking wasn't happening, she could barely mew or moan at this point. His mouth on her left her dizzy with lust.

His hands slid around her waist, and as quickly as she'd been dazed and confused, she snapped back to reality. He was touching her soft padding, her weak spot, her biggest vulnerability, and while he wasn't reeling in disgust, Becky's self-consciousness kicked into full gear. She wanted to pull away, to hide under covers. She was desperate for the voice to shut up, to leave her alone, but as his hands squeezed her flesh and then slid down to her full rear, which still had the courtesy of a skirt to cover it, she felt fat. *Not now, please not now.*

She didn't want to freak, didn't want to tell him, didn't want to show her vulnerabilities bubbling over, and did everything she could to turn off the voice that was telling her to suck it in, and to run and hide.

He seemed indifferent to the thoughts racing through her mind. He didn't know, couldn't know the panic that was creeping out of her, the anxiety that was filling her at this very second. She hated this side of herself, hated that she went there, and wanted to believe she was enough just as she was, but in this very moment…she didn't believe it herself.

Pulling back, "Maybe we should wait," she started, turning to reach for her shirt. Draping it over her shoulders, her fingers fumbling at the buttons, wanting to hide her body, her panic showed through the cracks of her armor.

"What's going on? Are you okay?" His voice was calm, reassuring, and as his fingers went up into her hair, he kissed her sweetly. "What just happened?"

"I don't know," she said, terrified he'd know her truth. She wasn't like the other girls he'd been with. She was round and full, soft, and curvy, and mostly fat.

She was fat and ugly, fat and desperate to hide from him, terrified he'd reel in disgust. She couldn't do this, not now...now yet. She needed to lose weight; she had to get serious about it this time, because how could he want to make love to somebody the size of a house.

"Shhh," he said, pulling her close. "What's going on?"

The look of a terrified doe was in her eyes. She couldn't say it, couldn't admit it, and yet she was horrified it was sneaking out. She wanted to be cool, calm, and collected. She wanted to act like it didn't matter, like she didn't care. Only she did. She was afraid it would matter to him too. She couldn't handle him making love to her and then never calling again. What if he saw her naked, completely naked and couldn't perform because he wasn't aroused. The pain would be scathing, too much to handle. She had to stop now before it became a reality.

"I'm just not ready," she stammered. Slipping her arms into the sleeves of her blouse, she felt relief in buttoning her shirt back up.

"Okay," he nodded. "It just feels like something happened. Is it me? Do you want me to leave? Have I upset you?"

"Oh gosh, no, it's not you. It's me," she said in a panic, not even realizing he might think it was him. The words were rushing out, in a rambling spill before she could stop them. "It's just what if you see me, and you can't get hard, and I'm not what you expected, and I'm soft and squishy, and not gorgeous like Jessica, and my body isn't great, and...."

His finger went up to her lips. "Shh," he started. "I am insanely attracted to you, Becky. I think you're beautiful. I know exactly who you are." He took his hand and placed it on Becky's. Taking it, he pressed it to his erection, still in his jeans. "Do you feel that? That's because of you."

Becky nodded, now embarrassed. "It's just," she started to cry softly. "Guys like you don't date girls like me."

"That's a mistake," he whispered. "If guys like me were smart, they would have started dating girls like you a long time ago. You are nothing but gorgeous to me."

She smiled softly, burying her head in his chest. Embarrassed by her moment of insecurity, she thanked him for soothing her nerves. "I'm sorry; I don't know what came over me."

"Do you need to stop? We don't need to do this. We can wait."

"I don't want to wait; I just don't want you to be disappointed."

Reed wrapped his arms tighter around Becky. "There's no way you could disappoint me," he reassured.

Looking up with tearstained eyes, she nodded. "Okay," she finally whispered.

His lips brushed tenderly against hers. "Why don't we take a break?" Leading her back to the living room, he sat on the sofa, and pulled Becky against him. Her back to his chest, they sat talking.

"I'm sorry," she said again. "I wanted this to be different."

"Don't apologize. Things will happen when they're supposed to."

Chapter 16

As the evening wore on they were saying their good-byes. With a kiss at the door, and another kiss, followed by another more passionate kiss, they both realized he wasn't leaving. Together they found themselves back in the bedroom. This time Becky was ready.

Their mouths moved from lips to necks, and then back to lips again. There was a hunger, a wild sensuality that had to be released. There was no other way.

Reed helped Becky with her shirt, slowly unbuttoning her once again, and as he helped her slide it off her of shoulders, he tenderly kissed her naked body. Pulling at the edge of his shirt, Becky nudged Reed. Lifting his shirt over his head, he stood before her solid and strong. She had to catch her breath, his was beautiful, like sculpted artwork, muscled and cut.

Reed's mouth on her breast had Becky dizzy with lust. She stood before him in only her panties. Climbing on the bed, Becky shifted out of her underwear and scrambled for safety beneath the covers.

As Reed removed his jeans, kicking off his shoes, he was left standing in his formfitting boxer briefs. They clung to his body, highlighting his very firm erection, which was fighting to get out. Sliding them down slowly, Reed climbed beside Becky.

This was about to happen - and his body, wow, his body. She was giddy with pleasure, and wanted nothing more than to feel him inside of her. As long as her mind didn't get in her way, this would be an amazing night. Hell, even if it got in her way, it had already been an amazing night.

Reed rolled up against her, and side by side, the couple got lost in heated kisses. Stopping long enough to brush her hair away from her face, he said what she didn't even realize she needed to hear, "I want to be here."

A small smile spread across her face, but before it could fully form, his mouth was back on her, their lips connecting.

Becky needed to taste him, wanted to lick his salty body, wanted to nibble on his neck, and pulling out of the kiss long enough to move lower she suckled on his neck, feeling his hot flesh against her lips. She wanted him, more than she'd wanted anybody in a long time.

Reed's hands were stroking her body, sliding up and down, stopping to squeeze and caress her round bottom. Each movement sent a rush through her body. She ached for more as his hands moved up along her hips and waist, before finding their way back to her breasts. His hands roamed, exploring each curve of her body, like he couldn't get enough.

Becky's own hands were taking in the landscape of his body, and as she ran them over his broad shoulders and down his firm biceps, she grinned. His body felt amazing under her touch. He was solid through and through. She was drawn to feel him, touch him, wanting to learn every bit of him.

Their mouths found one another again, their passion and hunger speaking volumes. Rolling Becky onto her back, Reed's mouth slowly moved down her body. Dotting kisses along her chest, his mouth stopped at her nipple. Sucking it between his lips, Becky moaned softly, his warm mouth catering to her needs.

Reed was a generous lover. He made Becky feel like she was the only person in the world, and it felt as if time stood still. He covered every inch of her body is wet, warm kisses, and then came behind with his fingers caressing and playing her like a well-tuned instrument.

As his fingers drew down across her stomach and to her naughty bits, Becky gasped softly. She was moist with desire, and there was no hiding it. His fingers toyed at her entrance, and as he breached her opening, Becky sighed, unable to hide the pleasure she was feeling.

Waves of arousal moved within in her as she reached her peak. Cresting and lapsing into a pile of melted butter under his touch, Becky drifted on the high of her orgasm. Reed smiled at the women beside him. Wearing a goofy grin, she leaned up and kissed her lover.

"I want to feel you inside of me," she whispered. She didn't have to ask him twice.

Climbing over Becky, Reed slowly penetrated his lover. With a long moan, feeling her warmth gripping him, he moved within her.

Falling in love was a dangerous thing in Becky's world. It meant she could get hurt, would most certainly get hurt, and the vulnerability left her nervous. As Reed thrust from above, Becky realized she was sliding down the slippery slope of love and if she wasn't careful, she'd end up getting her heart broken. Was it love, was it lust? She wasn't sure, but it sure felt like love. Maybe it was the endorphins rushing through her body, or the insanely attractive guy over here, or maybe, just maybe it was love. Was it too early for love, was it infatuation instead? She hated how the question rolled through her mind.

She wanted to be lost in the sensation, but her mind was too busy. She felt incredible, but more than anything she was scared. Now that she'd found love, she was terrified of losing it.

Did Reed love her, or was this simply a passing fancy? Would he allow himself to fall in love, or was he only looking for naked intimacy? Would she live up to his expectations, would he think she was a good lover, or was she lacking? Trying to shut her brain down seemed pointless, because the more she tried to ignore the thoughts the more they wanted to invade her mind.

Wrapping her legs around her lover, tilting her hips, she finally found herself back in the moment. He was art in motion, and looking up at him, watching him focused, watching him love her filled Becky's soul, filling a void that had been empty for way too long.

How could she love a man she'd barely dated? Sure they'd spent time together, and now this, but did that really equal love. Okay, so maybe it wasn't love, but it was something, something big like incredible like, insatiable like, fantastic like, aw hell, it felt like love. And while she was filled with warmth, she knew it was way too early to let words like that slip out. She'd scare him away, he'd look at her like some desperate freak, and then it would end before it even got started.

Reed's eyes were on her, and a soft smile spread across his face as he looked down. With a final thrust, he collapsed beside Becky. As he caught his breath and regained his composure, Becky bit her tongue forcing herself not to say the words that were creeping to the surface. *Don't say it, don't say it, don't say it.*

"That was amazing," she cooed instead, forcing herself to swallow the "L" word before she regretted it.

"You are amazing," he corrected. Turning up on his side, his stroked the side of her face with the back of his hand. Tender movements, and then leaning in, he softly kissed Becky's lips. "Thank you."

"Thank me," she started to giggle. "Me? Holy cow, thank you." She felt like a giddy schoolgirl with a crush.

Reed's smile got bigger, "I love how real you are."

"As opposed to?"

"It's that you're genuine. I've been around too many phony people in life, and genuine is refreshing."

"I was hoping you were about to say beautiful, sexy, insanely cute, but I'll settle for genuine," she said sarcastically.

"You're all of those things," he said, leaning back. "If I'm not careful, I'm going to fall in love with you."

"You say that like it's a bad thing," she mocked. *Shit, see, if she confessed love it would have been way too early. He's only thinking maybe he'll fall in love, and here I am ready to spill wordage before it's time.*

"I'm positive it's a wonderful thing, I just need to go slowly."

"I understand," she offered sympathetically. *Go faster, go faster, go faster!*

"I would like to take you on a proper date."

"I guess we did things backwards."

"There are no rules, but I'm not complaining that I'm currently in bed beside you," he grinned.

"Good thing, the customer service department is closed. Seriously, I'm pinching myself, Reed. I didn't expect..." she trailed off, suddenly feeling goofy.

"Didn't expect? Are you going to finish that sentence?"

"I guess I just didn't expect a guy like you would be interested in a girl like me."

"Why do you say that? You're the total package?"

"I'm an overstuffed package," she admitted grimly.

"You need to stop worrying about that. I'm here aren't I? I find you insanely sexy. You have to trust that. If I wasn't attracted to you, I wouldn't be naked in bed with you."

"I do like you naked in my bed," she smiled. "I'm sorry; I'm a little sensitive to it."

"It's okay to be sensitive to something, just don't let it own you."

"Wise words, I didn't realize you were more than a sexy body," she laughed.

"Oh, I see how it is, you only want me for my body," he teased.

"Dear goodness I want your body, but honestly Reed you make me smile. It's a nice feeling."

Leaning in, Reed kissed Becky's forehead. "You have a beautiful smile."

Blushing, Becky nuzzled into Reed, letting him wrap his arms around her and pulling her close.

After another round of intimacy, they found themselves drifting off to sleep, pressed tightly against one another.

On waking, Becky wanted to pinch herself, was she dreaming? Obviously not, he was still in her bed. As Reed stirred, Becky watched him. Opening his eyes, he looked over and saw his lover watching him.

"Good morning," he said quietly.

Becky's hand shot up over her mouth, "Morning."

"Is that some kind of covert operation? Are you afraid I'll read your lips?"

"Morning breath," she groaned. "Be right back," she said jumping out of bed. Why hadn't she thought of that earlier? The last thing she needed was for him to be all romantic and for her to be all icky.

"Come back," he requested, "hurry back to bed."

Brushing her teeth, Becky made the mistake of looking in the mirror. Bedhead! Her hair was pushed up all over, her mascara had smeared. She couldn't go back looking like this.

"I'm going to grab a shower," she called out from the bathroom. "I'll be out in a few minutes."

"Screw the shower, come back to bed."

Torn between being horrified at her morning appearance, and wanting to be in bed with Reed, she stood frozen in the bathroom, not sure what to do.

Finally, her brain moved forward, after what felt like forever. "Come take a shower with me," she called out playfully.

"Later," he called. "Come back to bed." Insistent she join him, she relented.

All she could see was her hair pushed up awkwardly and her mascara smeared. As she walked back to the bed, Becky was feeling about as unsexy as she could imagine.

Reed smiled.

"Are you laughing at me?" She asked defensively. "It's my hair isn't it?"

"Your hair is fine. I'm smiling because I'm happy." Reaching his arm out, "Come back to bed with me."

Climbing back onto the bed, she didn't know how he could see past her morning look, but astonishingly he barely seemed to notice.

"I want to do naughty things to your body," he flashed a schoolboy grin.

Shedding her apprehension, she decided to go with it. "Mmm, I'd like that."

Sweaty, the couple collapsed after another generous love making session.

"If you keep doing that, I'll never let you leave," Becky purred.

"You may have to kick me out."

Rolling out of bed, Becky got up and stretched. "Let me make you some breakfast. Would pancakes work? I could do French Toast if you prefer."

"Pancakes sound great."

Chapter 17

Becky couldn't wipe the grin off her face, and even after Reed left, she smiled all day long. Her cheeks hurt from smiling so big, but how could she not. Just about the hottest guy she'd ever met had spent the night in bed, with her, and they had amazing sex. She was giddy with joy over the turn of events and couldn't wait to talk to Sam, if she would answer her phone already.

When she finally got through, "Where have you been?"

"I met someone," Sam sang into the phone. "How did things go with Reed?"

"We did it," she squealed.

"Wow, really? Was it good? Was he big?"

"Sam! I'm not giving you details; just know that I'm smiling today, a lot!"

"That's great, Becks. So if you're not going to spill, can I? I had a totally hot night."

"Tell me, tell me."

"Isn't this interesting, you want my details, but won't share your own," she teased.

"You always share. I usually have nothing to share."

"You do now."

"I know, but this is different. This was special. I'm really falling for the guy."

"Fine, you don't have to kiss and tell. Anyway, at your dance the other night, I actually met someone."

"That's great, Sam."

"There's just one tiny detail I have to figure out."

"Such as," Becky groaned. There was always something.

"He's a little younger than me."

"How much younger?"

"A few years," she said, knowing she'd have to drop the truth soon. "Okay, so he's only nineteen, but he's really sweet."

"Nineteen?"

"Go ahead, I know you want to say something."

Becky bit her tongue. "If he's nice, and you're okay with him being that much younger…" she trailed off and let Sam fill in the rest of the details.

"I know, I know, but age shouldn't matter, right?"

"I guess," Becky hesitated. "It's just that at that age, they're at a different stage than where we are."

"I know," she sighed. "But he was cute and sweet, and he made me feel pretty, but it does kind of freak me out he still lives at home, and is still in school. Totally party age," she admitted. "Great, now you're making me rethink things."

"Sammy, I'm not saying he can't be a great guy, it's just that you'll be twenty-five in a few weeks, and you're probably in different stages of your life. You want to settle down at some point, and he's not even legal to drink," she said, bringing home her point.

"At least he's not jailbait."

"I'm not saying not to see him again; I'm just thinking you might be looking for different things."

"You're right," she sighed. "I keep latching onto guys, looking for something, but I think I'm afraid I'm never going to find it."

"The thing is, you sleep with them really fast, and never take time to get to know them."

"Okay, miss slutty slut, who just slept with Reed this weekend."

"Come on, that's different and you know it."

"Whatever, I didn't want to be the only one feeling whorish after my cougar moment."

"Sam, you'll meet somebody, you just have to stop jumping in bed with every guy who comes your way."

"I know I'm filling a void, it's just that I'd rather have somebody beside me, letting me believe for at least a moment in time I'm desirable and they want me."

"Sam, you're worth so much more than that."

"I know Becks, there's a piece of me that believes it, but the other piece is the one that goes too far. Maybe one day I'll break the pattern," she sighed. "Enough about me, tell me about Reed."

"I think I'm falling in love with him."

"Oh please, you? You're in love with him already. You fall fast and hard."

"Fine, so maybe I'm feeling stuff, I just don't know if it's love or lust at this point."

"Maybe it's a little bit of both."

"I need to put my brakes on. I always go too fast. It's just, I really like the guy, and I'm not sure how to control those feelings right now."

"One day at a time, my friend. One day at a time."

"So tell me about this new guy," Becky asked.

"I don't know, now I'm not as excited as I was earlier. He's nice and all, but he is only nineteen."

"Aw honey, I'm sorry. I didn't mean to deflate your fun. If you like the guy, then don't listen to me."

"I think it's that he was really into me, you know? I think it was an ego boost more than anything."

"Are you sure, or is it because I opened my big mouth?"

"I don't know, maybe he wasn't all that after all."

"I'm sorry, now I feel bad. I shouldn't have said anything."

"No, I count on you to keep it real. If I can't trust you to tell me the truth, who can I trust?"

"Forgive me for making you feel like a cougar?"

"Yeah, besides, I can't be considered a cougar until I'm older. I was simply testing the waters with a younger guy. So what's up with you and Reed, other than the big news that you totally did him?"

"We're going to go on a date, an actual date and see where it goes. I think we both really want things to work out, but with him coming out of a long term relationship, I didn't want him to jump too quickly."

"Becks, time has passed, let him move forward," she paused, "with you."

"I'm trying, I'm trying."

"When's your date?"

"We're going to go out Tuesday night. He wants to take me out for dinner."

"It's more than coffee," she said. "That's promising."

"Okay, I need to go. Oh, he's going to help me with my website, and I have applications to go through. I totally got more people to add to my database. I think by this time next year, I'll be in full swing. Until then, I'm sort of in beta mode, starting the process. Cross your fingers I get a few successful matches by then so I can promote my success rate!"

"You're totally going to do this, Becky. Look how far you've come."

"I know, I'm trying to be patient, but without a business loan, I'll have to do it slower."

"The bank made a big mistake," she sympathized. "Seriously, big girls need to date too."

"It wasn't about that, it was my lack of experience."

"Whatever, I just think they were biased."

"It'll be fine. I'll gain experience as I go, and then I don't have a loan to pay back. I just have to go really slow, because I can't afford to do too much."

"Oh, before I forget, I had a totally great idea. You should have a picnic at the park. It wouldn't cost anything except for food, and you could do another singles get together. You could arrange day trips for singles to places like museums, art galleries, parks, zoos, places that don't cost a lot."

"That's actually a great idea, thanks Sam."

"You're welcome," she grinned, feeling proud of her suggestion. "And if you happen to find a good looking, nice guy joining in, keep me in mind first." Clearing her throat to bring home her point, "But he should be at least over twenty-one. God knows I don't want to drink my wine alone."

"Good point. Okay, I'd better scoot. I have work to do."

When the phone rang later that evening, Becky smiled on seeing the caller ID. "Hi," her flirty voice snuck out.

"Hey," hearing him filled her soul.

"What are you doing?"

"Thinking about you," he said.

"Okay, if you keep talking like that, I'm going to melt into a puddle right here on the floor."

Reed laughed, "I wanted to see if you'd prefer French or Italian? I'm trying to decide where we're going on our first official big date."

"So you're not counting the coffee shop, this is the first big one? What about the dance?"

"Nope, we need to go on a proper first date. I'm thinking Italian, some pasta, some wine, and low romantic lighting."

"Are you trying to seduce me?"

"Very much so," he laughed.

"Because you could just stand in front of me and smile, and I'd be stripping off my clothes."

"I'd enjoy that, but at least let me take you out first. I'd love to spend more time getting to know you. I'll take you up on the stripping later that night."

She was incredibly happy, and nothing in the world could bring her down, or so she thought. Tuesday night had other plans for Becky and Reed.

Tearing through her closet, Becky pulled out a knee length navy dress. It was form fitting up top, but had a little extra flair at her hips and legs for a more flattering look. Pairing it with her black pumps and a simple silver necklace, she appraised her appearance. With a stroke of her signature red lipstick, and a quick retouch of her make-up, she was ready to go.

She was happy with what she saw from the front, but turning and seeing her profile in the mirror left her feeling a little self-conscious. She pulled in her stomach, and swore she'd need to start wearing shape wear soon, but this would have to do for now. At least her legs were still mostly shapely. She had thin ankles, but the closer you got to her pudgy knees, the more it became obvious she carried extra weight.

Reed showed up with a smile and flowers.

"You didn't have to," she started.

"You look great," he smiled, handing her the bouquet.

Turning to put the flowers in water, Reed reached out to touch. He couldn't not, her full, round ass sashayed as she walked, and before he could stop himself, his hands were on her.

"I lied," he laughed, "you look more than great."

"If you keep fondling my ass, we'll never get out of the house," she grinned.

"Would that be such a bad thing?"

"I wouldn't be complaining, but you made such a big deal about a date…" she trailed off, teasing him.

"You're right, you're right. Nutrition is good; you'll need your strength."

"Aren't you a tiger," she laughed. Finishing up, she turned toward Reed.

His eyes told her all she needed to know. He liked what he saw. As the relief washed through her, she let go of her critical side for the evening. She hated how she was harder on herself than she should be. So what if she carried a few extra pounds, she was still attractive. She wished she could hold onto that feeling more often.

Heading out to the car, the couple got in and drove to the restaurant Reed had picked out. It was an Italian place Becky was familiar with, but she hadn't been there in ages. Tuscany Grill offered brick oven pizza and lighter fare for lunch, while their dinners were hearty and sinfully delicious. She loved their veal parmesan.

Walking in, Reed reached down and held her hand, squeezing it gently. That tiny motion made Becky smile. They were here, together, as a couple. It felt surreal, the two of them dating. What had started as a silly crush on her side became a reality.

As the hostess seated them, and lit the small candle at their table, Becky sighed a little inside. This was happening, it was real. Sure, they'd already slept together, but this cemented the fact that there was something more, and it wasn't a mistake, some one time fling that ended after stars lined up perfectly one night in time.

Reed looked over at his date. Her soft, blonde hair left him wanting to run his fingers through it. He loved how silky it felt on his skin when he played with it the other night. He wondered what Becky was thinking, how things had changed, and if this was something good in her life. She was such a special girl, so down to earth, and was a breath of fresh air.

When she smiled, he couldn't help but smile back. Her face lit up, glowing with happiness. Her eyes danced with joy, and Reed knew he needed to spend more time with Becky Holgate, both dressed and undressed. Thinking back on their night the other day, Reed's mind flashed with snapshot images of her voluptuous body, and the thought alone had him feeling things below. There was stirring, and a semi-hardness happening, but that would have to wait.

As the waiter approached with the specials and to get their drink order, Reed shifted, trying to get his growing erection under control.

Ordering a bottle of wine, the couple lingered over their menus before making their selections.

Reaching across the table, Reed took Becky's hand, and tenderly stroked her fingers with his own. "I'm glad we're finally doing this."

"Me too," she answered softly.

They couldn't have known, couldn't have planned it, and as she marched up to the table, clearing her voice, Jessica stood with her hands on her hips, her voice full of hostility. "You've clearly moved on," she spat, and then turning to give Becky a once up and down, her voice changed gears. "Seriously, you could have me, and you're with someone like her?" She laughed, a cruel, mean laugh, and one that made Becky want to slide under the table. *Ignore her, ignore her.*

"Jessica, that's enough," Reed was short and firm.

"Enough? Yeah, I've seen just about enough. First you dump me, and then you end up dating a fat chick? What the hell, Reed?"

Turning to face Becky, "I'm sorry." Looking back at Jessica, "You're being rude, and you're not welcome here. I think you should leave."

"Oh, I'm not welcome here. The woman you were about to marry, but then decided to break up with months before our wedding is inconveniencing you. So sorry," she spit out sarcastically. "Don't let me interrupt your date, because you obviously have something more important to do than say marry the woman you proposed to."

"You're making a scene," his voice got tense. "This isn't the time or place."

"I'm so sorry," she dripped with annoyance. "Please forgive me for ruining your date with Bessy the Cow."

Her friend was visible perturbed but uncomfortable too. "Jess, come on, he's not worth your time."

"You're right," she finally said to her companion. "Let's go eat somewhere else. I'm not interested in a place that feeds losers and fat pigs," she snapped, before walking away.

Becky was horrified, crushed, and everything inside of her wanted to die. She wanted to slide under the table, become invisible, and pretend that none of this actually happened. Only it did.

Reed was apologetic, but like a schoolyard bully, Jessica had already done her damage. Becky could barely muster the courage to paste a smile to her face, to pretend like it didn't bother her, but she desperately wanted to run to the ladies room, lock herself inside one of the stalls and cry her eyes out.

What had started as an unbelievable experience, a date with a guy that felt leagues above her world, left her spinning in the gutter, wanting to vomit and hide.

"Maybe we should leave," Becky finally got out. The words were stuck in her throat, and she had to force them forward. She was choking on her misery, her complete embarrassment, and the humiliation appetizer his ex-girlfriend had just served.

Reed simply nodded and asked for the check. He couldn't undo this, couldn't peel away her pain, couldn't unsay the words that were said, and Becky realized in that moment, that maybe this wasn't meant to be.

Her vulnerability crumbled beneath her, and took her soul with it.

She was silent in the car, as Reed apologized over and over again. What was meant to be a magical evening had turned into a nightmare, and one Becky wouldn't soon forget.

Getting out of his car, he walked her to the door. Leaning in to kiss her goodnight, Becky stopped him. "I don't think this is going to work out. I know it wasn't you, but there's still a lot of stuff for you two to work out."

Reed was frustrated. "There's nothing for me to work out, and I'm sorry you had to sit through that, but I want to be here. Don't think for a minute that this changes anything for me."

Becky looked at Reed, and he saw it in her eyes. The slow painful death she felt tonight. "I'm sorry," she said and let herself in, closing the door on the man that she thought would be joining her in bed tonight.

Becky was numb. Kicking off her heels, she walked to the sofa and curled into a ball. In the privacy of her home, with no eyes on her, she cried her eyes out.

The sting of the words, the embarrassment of it happening in front of Reed, and the anger at Jessica for not only taunting her, but making a scene and ruining her date all tangled together into one large heap.

Letting go of Reed meant Jessica won, but she was too horrified to spend time with him. Not now, maybe not ever. He'd always hear her words, calling her Bessy the Cow and a fat pig, and he'd always know that he was shunned for dating a big girl.

Becky cried for her size, hating herself even more than usual in that moment, and felt pathetic and lonely. When her anger finally kicked in, she started to feel better for a few moments, but it didn't last long. She bathed in her self-pity and lingered in the sorrowful feelings.

It wasn't until she was buried under her covers in bed later that night that she started to realize that Reed chose her. He had Jessica, but he chose her. Why couldn't she see that earlier? She'd already won. If Becky walked away from Reed, that was letting Jess win, and there was no way in hell she'd let that bitch ruin things for her.

Becky adored Reed, and she'd be damned if some mean lady was going to get in her way. Becky deserved better, and letting the bully win wasn't the answer. Sure she had a little extra weight on her body, but since when does a number on the scale dictate who you are?

She was a smart, fun, and good person, and that should count for something. And she was pretty, so what if she carried a few extra pounds, she was still a pretty girl, and Reed had certainly let her know he was attracted to her.

She was more than her body, she was a complete package. No way in hell was she going to let Jess get under her skin. Sure she got to her, broke her down, hit her vulnerability, but Becky was going to come back stronger. *Push me down little bitch, but I'll stand right back up. Fuck her.* She was better than that, and she refused to let her win. She might have ruined their date, but she didn't have to ruin their relationship.

Finding her courage and strength once again, Becky called Reed. "I'd like a redo."

"A redo?"

"Yes, I'd like another date," she said quietly. "Could we try again?"

"You're sure?"

"Very."

"I'd love to take you out again. I'm so sorry she ruined the evening."

"You don't need to apologize for her actions."

"Would you like to try again tomorrow?"

"Very much."

"I'm glad you called," he said.

"Me too."

Becky went to sleep feeling one hundred times better than she'd felt earlier that evening. She fought back and she won. There was no way she was going to let a bully dictate her relationship.

Chapter 18

Their second date went much smoother, and this time when Reed went to kiss Becky goodnight, she invited him in. Every time he kissed her, she melted. She loved being in his arms, feeling his sweet lips against hers. Walking in, they barely made it through the door, when they were back together, sharing in intimate moments. Closing the door, Reed pressed Becky to it, pulling her hands up over her head. His mouth worked over her neck, with soft caressing kisses, that had Becky wanting to strip off her clothing.

Breaking apart only long enough to head toward her bedroom, they stopped midway, stopping in their tracks.

"Oh crap," she said, staring at her sassy cat who was now lovingly or not so lovingly humping Mr. Bunny, a stuffed rabbit Becky had tucked on a shelf. Not only had the cat gotten up to the shelf, but he assaulted Mr. Bunny by knocking him to the floor and was now flagrantly making passionate love to the stuffed rabbit. The bunny was a silent partner, not really participating. His happy little sewn on smile was still on his face, almost making him look like he was enjoying it.

"Oh Bella," Becky moaned, "Scoot, you," she said, chasing the kitty off of the plush rabbit. "I'm sorry you had to see that," she said flatly.

Reed could only laugh. "I think you've managed to break it up, allowing your stuffed rabbit to keep some of its dignity."

"Mr. Bunny has no dignity," she grinned. "He's a total slut, but I prefer that my cat doesn't hump him in front of company. Mr. Bunny actually likes it, and has on many occasions spent the evening with the horny Bella."

"So you're saying that Mr. Bunny wants it?"

"Hey, Bella can be quite a dick tease, all flirty and sexy, bathing in front of Mr. Bunny. I'm just saying I think it goes both ways, but I do expect them to refrain from that kind of activity when there's company."

Reed pulled Becky into his arms, his face wearing a smile, "You're a piece of work."

"A good piece or work, or like a slightly twisted, bent out of shape piece of work?" She teased.

"Slightly? Oh, I'd say a very twisted, tangled, and a messed up piece of work. Have I mentioned that's my favorite kind?"

"You have not," she said, eyes opened wide, feigning shock. "What a coincidence."

"A wonderful coincidence if you ask me." Reed kissed Becky, saving small talk for later.

She whispered, "Breathless, you leave me breathless."

"Aroused is what you do to me," he answered, taking her hand and placing it on his firm erection still safely tucked away in his pants.

"I believe I shall take you to bed," she grinned, and pulled him behind her.

"Bed is a good place to be."

"Especially when it's with you," she grinned.

Naked and under the covers, the couple made love.

In the afterglow of the moment, Becky slipped, "I love you, Reed." Her hand shot up to her mouth, clasping over it.

Reed heard the words. His head spun toward Becky in slow motion. What should he say, how should he react? He cared about the girl, but he wasn't ready to go there, and in a heated moment of panic, he stroked her cheek and said, "That's sweet."

**

"That's sweet?" Sam whined into the phone. "That's all he said."

"I blew it; I didn't mean to say it. Sure it's okay to think it, but it's too soon. We both know it's too soon, but I was high on endorphins, drifting on the afterglow of an orgasm, and before I could stop myself, the words came out. I mean, I'm pretty sure I love him, and before I could even contemplate it anymore, it was a done deal."

"What did you say after he flubbed? I wonder what he was thinking."

"He probably freaked the hell out is what he did. He didn't flub, I did. I was in a panic and apologized, trying to take it back, but there it was sitting between us like dead air. I totally made the experience weird."

"Sorry Beck, I'm not sure what to tell you. And holy shit, what's with Jessica? What a bitch."

"I know. I wanted to call you that night, but I didn't have it in me. I was like a wilted flower, all sobbing uncontrollably and curled up under the covers."

"I don't blame you, though I would have been pissed. Don't you dare let her win, not a bitch like that."

"I know; that's why I got over myself and called him back, which landed me in this mess."

"What's the big deal, so he knows you have strong feelings, it could be worse."

"I'm just afraid he'll feel trapped. He just got out of a long term relationship, and I'm already throwing *I love you* his way. I didn't mean to, it just slipped. Now he's going to hear that every time he looks at me, and I can't take it back. I mean, sure I could say it was a mistake, but I didn't say it was a mistake in that moment. Shit Sam, it was only our second date, and the first was ruined."

"Okay, so technically it was your second date, but you'd gotten together before that, and you've known him for a while. It's not like he's a total stranger. Do you love him?"

"Yeah, I think I do. I mean, I guess. It feels like love, but maybe it's just lust. But yeah, I think I'm in love with the guy."

"How do you know it's love, and not just infatuation? You were kind of blown away when he said he was interested. Maybe it's more fascination and hero worshipping."

"Hero worshipping, seriously, work with me here. I mean, it feels real."

"Okay, so let's figure this out. What kind of real is it? Like you want to have his babies real, or like if he lost a testicle, didn't have a job, and couldn't have sex anymore because he gained five hundred pounds and his asthma stopped him from having hot sex, you'd still be by his side real?"

"What kind of question is that?"

"You know what I'm saying, don't be coy. If you just want babies, it's still infatuation. If you'd sit by his side as he got his testicle removed and gained a bunch of weight and couldn't find his dick to put it inside of you anymore, would you still want him?"

"Sam!"

"What? It's a legitimate question. You don't have questions like that to measure things?"

"Not that extreme."

"Seriously, there's a method to my madness. Picture this, he can't find his winky anymore, it's hidden between his legs, he can't reach, he's out of breath when he tries, and the most you can do is blow him, like that's it. He might diddle you time to time so you aren't feeling too hopeless in the sex department, and he doesn't want you straying. Would you still be there?"

Becky sighed, going with the flow of the conversation. "Fine, yes, I'd still be with him. He's more to me than some hard body to have sex with. I really like the guy. I like talking to him, laughing with him, and learning more about him."

"Nice. I think you may very well be in love, Becks. Now if you could find me a guy like that…"

"The one that can't find his wiener, or someone to love," she laughed.

"Hey, I'll help him find his wiener if he's awesome."

"There's some guy named Jonathon that I believe you thought was pretty great, but you couldn't spend time with him because you didn't like his laugh."

"You're right, I'm shallow. I totally want someone who can find their winky and laughs like a guy. Not like a girl, Becky. I swear to you, it's a little disconcerting."

Becky laughed. "Fine, but I think you should give the guy another chance. You had a good time."

"You're not listening. I had a good time until he laughed. I had visions of teenage girls in my mind because his laugh sounded like a schoolgirl giggling, not exactly sexy. What part aren't you getting?"

"And yet you still slept with him."

"I'm a lost cause," she sighed.

"Not totally lost, because I'm going to steer you in the right direction. Go out with Jonathon again and try giving him another chance."

"Come on, Becks, that's not fair. Besides, he's not exactly banging down my door to see me again."

"Maybe he thinks you laugh like a guy," she teased.

"Great, we can be a freak show together, that's what you want for your best friend? Oh my gosh, I totally don't laugh like a guy, do I?"

Becky rolled her eyes, "Sam, you're a twisted one."

"I thought that's why you liked me."

"I think it's our history. I've known you too long and you know all my secrets."

"I'll never tell anyone, they're safe with me, unless of course you set me up with a guy that laughs like a girl."

"Fine, I'll drop it. Anyway, I've got to go."

"Hey Becks, sorry things didn't go how you wanted."

"Thanks, it'll be fine. He'll dump me and I'll be forced to settle for guys that laugh like girls."

"And I'll be some old spinster with cats that are addicted to kitty nip and no guy because I had stupid ass requirements."

"So you'll give Jonathon some thought?"

"I didn't say that."

"Just think about it. You said you had a great night."

"Fine, I'll think about it."

"Love you Sammy, but I've got to go."
"Bye."

Chapter 19

Business was picking up with the addition of more applications, and Becky was able to set up a couple of people. Her first match was still dating, though her second didn't go over as well. At least she had some success with her first couple. There wasn't exactly a wedding in the works yet, but it was still early and both were pleased. The couple was going to invest more time getting to know one another.

As Becky's phone buzzed, she mindlessly reached down for it, knocking her diet soda to the ground. "Crap, hello?"

"Lovely greeting, do you greet your boyfriend that way?"

"Hey, Sam, give me a second. I spilled my drink," she said running to the kitchen to grab a towel. Cleaning up the spill she said, "Besides, he's not my boyfriend."

"What? You said you loved him, and you don't consider him your boyfriend."

"Well, it's not like I'm seeing anybody else, but I don't know if he thinks we're exclusive. I haven't brought it up, and he hasn't either which I'm taking as a sign."

"That's not good. Maybe you should mention it."

"I want to, but it's so awkward. What do I say?"

"You'll figure it out. You never like my suggestions."

"Right, but your suggestions amuse me and teach me what not to say."

"Thanks, Becks, thanks."

"What's up?"

"Well, I thought about what you said, and I called Jonathon."

"Get out! Really?"

"He seemed pleased to hear from me, and we got to talking. I was thinking maybe we could go out again, and then he did it."

"Oh, please no."

"He laughed and reminded me how incredibly unsexy it was. Seriously, if you could hear him you'd understand. He's a great guy, but I couldn't live my life with that."

"You're going to die old and alone, Sammy."

"Better alone than hating my husband's laugh," she countered.

"Good point."

"Anyway, I also had something else happen that you might find interesting."

"Really, what happened?"

"I ran into Brady at the pet supply store, and he asked me out to lunch."

"Did he now?"

"Only, I had a two o'clock appointment and it was already one, so I had to pass, but we're going to go out this Sunday."

"That's great. Is it just friendly, or are you thinking you might be interested in him again?"

"I'm holding judgment, but decided I'd go out with him one more time. Only I'm holding off on sex. Just because I slept with him, doesn't mean I'm going to sleep with him again. I've got a new four date rule."

"This is the first I'm hearing about it, and what about his sexual skills that were you less than thrilled with? Four dates is good."

"I'm going to overlook it for now, maybe it was performance anxiety. Besides, it's not like he can't improve with a little help. We barely knew each other. And I'm sharing my new rule with you now, aren't I? If I have three successful dates with a guy, then I'll sleep with him on the fourth date, but not a moment before."

"Do you think you can hold out that long?"

"I'm going to try. How are things going with Reed?"

"They're going, I mean, there's the whole not sure if we're exclusive thing, but he is cooking dinner for me this weekend. I'll be staying at his place Saturday until Sunday, so don't call me unless it's an emergency."

"Are you going to bring up the exclusive thing?"

"I'm not sure."

"Becks, maybe he thinks you guys already are exclusive, but just hasn't said anything. You've been seeing a lot of him."

"Right, that's how I think. I only want to date one guy at a time, but I just don't want to feel like a fool if he's thinking about dating other people."

"You've got this, sister, just come out and say what you're thinking."

"I guess," Becky sighed. "I'll have to bring it up eventually. I just don't want to spoil the weekend."

"Maybe it will make it that much more special."

"We can hope."

Finishing their conversation, Becky got back to the business of her dating agency. Between the applications she had so far, and the event she held, she was sure she'd have a solid database soon enough. With one more event in mind, she wanted to put together a park picnic for singles. She hoped with enough advertising she'd bring in more potential clients.

She didn't have a lot of money for the actual event, but she could grill hotdogs and bring chips and pretzels. If she made it BYOB it would even be more affordable. Lastly, she'd set up stations like Frisbee, croquet, and other outdoor activities. Her biggest hurdle right now was getting her name out there and letting people know she was building a matchmaking business.

Becky spent the night playing with wording for an ad, and after finally finishing called it a night. With the weekend coming up quickly, the rest of her spare time was focused on figuring out how to bring up the topic of an exclusive, monogamous relationship with Reed. She didn't want to push him away by being needy, but she also didn't want to be one of many.

Reed was making a prime rib with red bliss potatoes and fresh asparagus for dinner Saturday night. Becky was impressed with his ability in the kitchen, because while she could get around and make a few things, she was certainly no chef herself.

She played out the conversation in her head a million times, and every single time she felt desperate. "What do you think about idea of being exclusive?" "How do you feel about dating other people?" "I want you to know, I'm not seeing other people." She groaned, going back and forth, trying to figure out how to approach the topic. Maybe she should just let it go, and let him bring it up when he's ready.

It made her stomach turn, the thought of him possibly being with somebody else. But, what if he had wild oats to get out of his system after being with the same person for so long? Dropping her head, she decided that it would be up to him. She obviously wasn't going anywhere. She already gave up the secret that she was in love with him. She cringed on remembering his response - "that's sweet" and wished she could have a do over.

When the weekend finally rolled around, Becky picked up a bottle of wine to go with dinner. It was the least she could do, since he went through the effort of cooking for her. Showing up, she smiled on seeing his face. She smiled every time she saw him. It didn't matter the occasion, simply being around him was enough to make her happy.

"It's great to see you," he said, taking the bottle of wine from Becky and heading into the kitchen to get glasses. "I wanted to talk to you about something. I've been thinking a lot about what you said the other day, and how I handled it."

"Oh, you don't have to," she stammered, realizing he was jumping right into the hot topic. She went into a full fledge panic, knowing there was no way to avoid it now. With it tossed into the fire, she suddenly felt embarrassed all over again.

"I feel like there's this divide, and I want to address it."

Becky blushed, realizing there was nowhere to hide.

"The thing is, I really like you," he said, pausing for a moment, "I'm just not there yet. We're still getting to know each other."

"I rushed it, I didn't mean to say it, the orgasm, I was lost in the moment, it slipped," she rambled, trying to get out of the awkward situation. She was squirming and needed to stop this conversation dead it its tracks.

"I wanted to be honest and up front with you. I can't make any promises, and I have to put that out there."

"I'm not looking for a promise." Becky was fumbling, fidgeting, this was too uncomfortable. As much as she liked him, she realized they were in different places emotionally. She felt like a fool.

Taking Becky's hand, he kissed it. "I'd like to continue getting to know you better. I'm hoping we'll be spending a lot of time together, but I need to go slowly. I just got out of a relationship, and though I know it was for the best, I want to make sure you don't pay for my mistakes. If I jump from one relationship to another so quickly, I won't have time to process my true feelings."

"Wow, you sound mature," she mumbled.

"I'd like to think I'm doing right by you. You're a special girl, and I don't want you to be some rebound that just fills a gap. I'm hoping you're more than that, but I can't promise where we'll end up, just that I'd like to walk the path with you."

Becky nodded, not sure what to say. They were great words, wonderful words, hell, they were wise words, but in that very moment, she was stuck. She didn't know what to say.

"Dinner smells great," she said meekly.

"Are you okay?" Reed was looking at her. There was something else. "Did I hurt your feelings?"

Becky shook her head, "No, not at all." She was torn, not sure what to do, what to say. She wanted to feel romantic and sexy, but all she felt was rejected. He didn't even reject her, but it like he was letting her down gently, without even breaking up with her. He would eventually though – guys like Reed don't date girls like her. She swallowed hard. "I need to use the bathroom, if you'll excuse me." She kept her composure long enough to close the bathroom door behind her, and then sinking to the floor, caught her breath.

Why did it feel worse than it was? He said she was special, but why did it feel like he was buffering a blow. She just had to keep it together long enough to get out of there. This wasn't going to work; there was no way it could work. He wasn't feeling it. Becky was ready to go forward, but Reed was still doggy-paddling and wanted to stay in place. They weren't compatible, this was a mistake. She'd never have matched the two of them in her business, because let's face it, they don't belong together. *You're just a silly girl with a crush. Let it go – let him go.*

She lost track of time and didn't want to go back out there. She declared her love for him, and he shut her down. He couldn't promise a future, just a good time. Her ears were ringing, hearing his tone, all condescending, like he had to pander to her, afraid she'd break down.

Standing up, she looked in the mirror and ran her fingers through her hair. *You can do this, enjoy the evening and then leave. You're going to get hurt, because yes Becky Holgate, you are most certainly in love with Reed Amwell, but he can't promise you anything, and that means he'll be seeing other people. Don't be one of many, don't do it.*

Taking a deep breath, she let herself out of the bathroom and walked to the kitchen to join Reed. Pasting a fake smile on her face, she sat at the table. "Can I help with anything?"

"No, it's just about ready," his head was down, as he bent to remove the prime rib from the oven. Placing it on the stove top, he turned around and grinned, "It's done." Looking at Becky, he knew something was wrong. It was in her face, that wasn't her real smile, and her eyes were flat.

Sliding his oven mitts off, he went over to sit with Becky. "What's the matter, sweetheart?"

"Nothing, why do you ask?"

"Because that's not your real smile," he answered softly.

"What are you talking about? It's the same smile I always wear."

"No," he said quietly, "it's not. When you smile your face lights up, and your eyes do this sparkling thing, sort of dancing, and you get the cutest dimple."

Becky looked down.

"What's going on?"

"It's not important, besides dinner is ready."

"Dinner can wait."

Becky looked up at Reed. "I don't do the date a lot of people thing well. I guess I wanted to ask you if wanted to be exclusive, but your big speech tonight sort of shuts that down. I'm not sure I can handle dating you, knowing you're out with other women."

"Wait a minute, what made you think I was thinking of dating other women?"

"You're afraid I'll be a rebound, and you can't make promises, because you want to be with other people."

"Whoa, you're adding words there. I never said anything about other women. I just don't want to promise you forever before we truly know. Becky, I love being around you, and I only intend to date you. Hell, when I was with Jessica, I knew there was something special about you. I don't want to rush things, because I want to do things right."

"Like dating for a while, before we sleep together," she teased softly.

"Okay, well, could you blame me? You've got that luscious body, and you're adorable."

"You think I'm luscious?"

"Have I not made that obvious? Listen, I like you. I like you a lot. I just need to be sure before I can use those words. They're big words, and when I say them, I mean them. It just takes me a little longer to get there. We've only known each other a short while."

"I felt like such a fool. I didn't mean to say it. I think I was just in the moment," she cringed. "I think it was lust more than love, not that I don't like you a lot."

"Whatever it is, we'll figure it out, but let's do it one step at a time, okay?"

Becky nodded.

"And yes, I'm a one woman man. I like that in my women too, so if we're going to keep doing this, I'd appreciate that in return."

"Like exclusive?" She grinned, realizing what he was saying.

"Like exclusive," he confirmed.

The smile that lit up her face couldn't hide her relief and joy. It was the very same smile that Reed had fallen for that first day he met her, that and her incredible laugh.

Chapter 20

Thankfully it was a sunny day, and as Becky got ready for the event, gathering up the last of her things, Reed showed up. "Let me carry that for you," he said taking one of the heavier bags.

"I'm so excited; I think we might get a nice turn out."

"With the website finished, you can send people right to the database to enter their applications now. You'll be able to see everything from the administrator side, but it will cut out the need for paper applications. I even made it a mobile friendly site for tablets and phones."

Becky leaned in kissing Reed, "Thank you so much for that. It looks amazing. I never could have done that on my own. Did you bring your camera?"

"It's in the car. I'll be sure to get some great candid shots to add to your singles event page."

"You're the best." Yelling over her shoulder, "Bella behave."

Heading out to Reed's car, they loaded up the stuff for the picnic.

When Sam showed up with Brady, Becky smiled. This would count as their second date without sex, and if Sammy could hold out, she might make it to a third. She was trying to go sex-free for the first few dates, thinking if she slowed things down maybe something would stick. Brady seemed happy as a clam, so Becky figured it was working just fine.

Pulling her aside, "How's it going? I'm so proud of you!"

"I caved before coming over."

"What?"

"It is what it is," she shrugged. "Besides, I think I like him more than I thought I did."

Becky rolled her eyes, "I knew it."

"Seriously, you didn't think I'd last?"

"Samantha, how long have I known you?"

"Okay, Mrs. I slept with Reed before going on an official date."

"Whatever," she said, grinning, heading back to greet the new people arriving.

Reed snapped candid shots of the day, though he was pretty sure he took more pictures of Becky than anyone. Becky smiling, Becky laughing, Becky looking beautiful…he was pretty sure he was in love. Seeing her through his lens made things crystal clear. She was most definitely the one that made his heart beat faster. He knew she was his future, and he had every intention of making her his wife. Funny, how he had to be pushed into a commitment in the past, but with Becky his future couldn't start soon enough. Reed smiled and snapped pictures of his future bride.

THE END

Thank you for choosing an Ava Catori story. If you'd like to see a full list of Ava Catori titles, visit AvaCatori.com, or check your favorite e-book retailer. At the website, you can also sign up to be notified of new titles. If you enjoyed this story, please take a moment to leave a review, so others can see if this is a story they might enjoy.

Some other titles by Ava Catori:

Shady Cove: New Girl in Town

(New Adult Romance) Can a big city girl go country? Jenna's life grinds to a halt after her brother's suicide. With her college funds non-existent and her future plans put on hold, she's forced to relocate to a sleepy town. Just when her entire world is crumbling, she meets Benji Preston, a local guy she doesn't expect to fall for. He's not even her type! A harmless flirtation quickly escalates into something more. The only catch? He's the same guy her cousin has been harboring a crush on for ages. With tongues wagging and jealousy dogging her every step, Jenna has to decide what's more important; her heart or her family ties

Compulsive Desires

Is it infatuation or love? Sophie Samuels was in love. Well, okay, maybe it was lust, but who wouldn't be? Bear Trevor, the Bear Trevor, famous adventurer and male model had just fallen in her lap.

It started with a conversation, and then a wicked one night stand, but now Bear was asking for more. The only problem was that Sophie was confused by what she was feeling.

Were her growing feelings real, or was she simply infatuated with the handsome star? Sifting through the details of their fling, Sophie is forced to admit her new obsession may be just that - an obsession. Can Bear convince Sophie that they could be much more together, or will Sophie realize it's not love after all?

Quality Candy: Running from the Past

Candace Brown had a past, one that she kept well hidden. Now that she had snagged a promotion at work, she was feeling pretty good about herself - that is until Ryan enters the pictures.

Ryan Gentry knows Candy's past. In fact, she's the one who took his virginity ten years ago. Only seeing her unexpectedly throws him off of his game, and he finds himself attracted to the girl he once knew.

Avoiding Ryan becomes Candace's goal, until he lands smack in her office. Can she continue to push him away when chemistry starts to brew? Accepting Ryan into her world means accepting her past, and that's one thing she's still running from.

How far would you run to escape your past, and what would you sacrifice to keep a firm grip on your future? Candace Brown is about to find out.

Made in the USA
Middletown, DE
08 August 2017